Glimmer of Love

Confession of Love

Shelley M. Jenkins 2017

Simply Unique
Writing Diva Books, LLC

WEDDING DAY

My white veil waved from side to side
Two horses galloping through the path
I'm anxiously waiting to see my groom
While I enjoy this Cinderella carriage ride
I anticipate –
On becoming a gorgeous bride,
And walk beside my groom side by side
For the rest of my life
Love, honor, and respect him as his
We crossed a small bridge
Like the one that we overlapped when we went on our first date
The sounds of the calm water flowing through the river
Love followed us as we discovered each other
We built our dreams together;
We promised to love one another forever
Hollyhock flowers covered the venue
White doves flying in the wind
The tears I cried just continued
My companion waits at the altar
With his best man; his name is Walter
I stepped down from the carriage
Prepared to join my fiancée in marriage
My white ballroom gown tapped the floor
I took a deep breath as my groom opened the carriage doorMy
future husband walked me down the long intriguing path
We cried and talked about how we first met
Rose petals laid on the ground
The flower girls tossing them about
My heart traveled into another world;
This is true love
Each step, I took seemed like a mile

Shelley Jenkins

Still crying; the tears are still pouring
My heart is humming by the groom's smile
My father takes over then we walk down the aisle arm and arm
He gave me away and hugged me firmly
My groom stood at the altar;
I held my friend, my lover, my protector's hand
I can hear the crowd mumbling, "Amen!"
I pinched my arm to see if I was dreaming
Because this perfect picture is too bright and gleaming
This sensational ceremony has me raving
My husband to be love has stunned me
His name paved into my heart;
Personally, engraved Jason my Darling
I gazed into his eyes
Then I utter my wedding vows
Our passion is finalized
We say I do, and we are no longer two—attribution

DEDICATION

When I was a teenager around sixteen, I remember hearing bits and pieces about domestic violence happening very close to home. That's when I discovered; it does exist.

I asked my mother repeatedly, "Tell me your story and I will write your book;" however, she never told me her story, but I wrote this book.

She is a great mother! I thank my uncle and auntie (Hosea's parents) who assisted my mother with raising me when my father wasn't there.

I thank everyone who played an essential part in my life; you are the reason why I am — where I am today, and who I have become.

I dedicate this book to domestic violence victims. I am sure everyone is acquainted with a victim of domestic violence in some way. It could be you, a friend, a family member, a co-worker, a neighbor, or an in-law.

I am not a counselor, therapist, or legal representative, so always seek professional help. This book was solely written to inform domestic violence victims that although every minute of the day – the week; may appear to be dreary and hopeless, there is always a safe way out of an abusive relationship.

This fairy-tale ending may or may not be your story or your outcome, but the point of the narrative is to assure you that there is a healthier start to a new beginning.

If you are considering suicide, you may want to rethink that thought. Seek professional help, guidance because I guarantee you, no matter how bad you may think your life may be, there is always someone who would argue your point. Yes, it will be a few distressing days, but I am sure there will be many great ones too.

I am speaking from the heart, but I am aware that there are true stories and real victims. Parts of this story are genuine. I know people who have experienced what you are battling with the beatings, the isolation, the bullying, the fear, and the pain — the desperate screams inside for one person to notice your distress.

The strangulation that's not only physical; however, mentally, your space may be so – restrained, or your freedom may be so – limited that you feel as if you cannot breathe. The outcome does not have to be unfortunate.

Every victim that I have been acquainted with states the same thing if there are no changes for the best, and you continue to be a victim of domestic violence daily find the safest way out, speak with professional help or contact law enforcement, they are there to serve and protect you.

I realize speaking out is a hard decision. You may be a little embarrassed because you never thought it would be you. Someday, I may have to say, "I never thought it would be me." There are a lot of graves filled with victim's who never thought that it would be them.

You probably have a million legitimate and convincing reasons why you should stay in that violent situation with your spouse, lover or your mate; however, I am sure there are many victims' laying in the graveyard that never had a chance to get away, speak out, or tell their story. Please do not become that victim.

Law enforcement cannot serve or protect you if you do not call for service or ask for help. Please pray and seek advice before you become just a memory!

Contents

Title Page
Poem
Dedication
Contents
Copyright Page
Acknowledgment
Chapter...................1
Chapter...................2
Chapter...................3
Chapter...................4
Chapter...................5
Chapter...................6
Chapter...................7
Chapter...................8
Chapter...................9
Chapter...................10
Chapter...................11
Chapter...................12
Chapter...................13
Chapter...................14
Chapter...................15
Chapter...................16
Chapter...................17
Chapter...................18

Shelley Jenkins

ACKNOWLEDGMENTS

An exclusive, thanks to God – Jesus! Thank you, God, for allowing me to bless others with significant words of love, compassion, hope, or inspiration.

The Illustrator, Hosea Moseley who created the beautiful picture and the lovely title, you are a great artist.

Unique, thanks to you! The book cover touched my heart and positively influenced me to push a little harder.

Hosea supported me every step of the way, without his motivation, I am confident that I would still be on page one. He is a great friend, family member, and a superb artist who brought my thoughts to life through his picture.

I hope you enjoy this book. It is my first novel, but hopefully not my last.

The editor, Steve Fortosis, who analyzed, corrected, and assisted me with putting this book together.

"Thanks, Fortosis" for being so patient with me and doing such a brilliant job. I was reading the book, and at one point, I was at astonished, and it caught my attention.

I enjoyed the dramatic touches! Fortosis also encouraged me and complimented me on my work when I doubted myself.

Parents, siblings, in-laws, cousins, friends, co-workers, and the rest of my family thank you again for your support and encouragement! I love you!

I thank the kind man "Mr. B" and the person who assisted me in obtaining my licenses very quickly. Thank you!

Shelley Jenkins

I thank Mrs. Dees, who read my manuscript and stood by me as I annoyed her daily. Thank you for being a great friend!

I thank my cousin, Danette Moseley, as well for directing me and helping me organize the book.
I thank everyone who read every boring poem that I have ever written, which led me into this direction.

I thank each of my supervisors, who corrected my reports; your critique improved my writing skills. I thank everyone who read the book and gave me their input. I appreciate you.

Someone close to my heart said, "You have a way with words." I hope that you share the same intensity.

CHAPTER *1*

atherine –

January 12, 2011

My mother, Pamela Roosevelt, told me her story; it was the replica of my life. I was treading in her footsteps.

We peeped through an identical – hazy, shattered, hideous mirror. Our lives pounded into pieces by love.

However; it was funny – how we needed to be, introduced to that same love again. So, it could cure our broken hearts.

I recall sitting on the edge of my boss' bed. Thinking – what happened to my great life? How did I end up here?

I was trembling, heartbroken, and in pain, nearly beaten to death. Earlier, I'd been raped by my boyfriend.

I was sitting on the bed contemplating if I should return home to him; however, I was too afraid of the bastard.

He was an obsessive, abusive, dangerous lunatic who held me hostage through fear. I was afraid to leave him.

My mother walked into the room. She fell apart when she saw me.

It was devastating the look in her wounded eyes. I could see the alertness inside of them.

She said, "Katherine Roosevelt look at you," her eyes filled with water. Tears started to run down her cheeks. It must have been contagious, since, tears began to roll down my cheeks as well.

"Baby let me tell you my story."

"What story, mother?"

I was in too much pain to move, too embarrassed to speak, and too ashamed to look into my mother's eyes. However, she had her confessions.

Pamela –

Katherine, I was born on December 05, 1950. I was a happy child.

Pretty much like you, but things happened – life happened. The roll of the dice changed – my luck changed.

I was bitter, furious, and I had self-pity bolted inside of me. Baby, please don't become my reflection; it's foggy.

At a young age, I believe you were twelve. I told you to never fall in love. I was firmly against it, but I never told you why I forbad that word in our household.

I was born in Michigan, a pre-teenager; thirteen when my parents died – I died. My mother passed away first due to an illness. A couple of months later, my father passed away.

People believed he died because of love; he was love sicken over my mother. I thought the same theory.

I was lonely – abandoned by everyone. I resided with other family members going from house to house, laying my head down anywhere that I could sleep. I was homeless. I wanted a place of my own that I could call home.

Hungry and desperate to eat, not starving for food, but, for attention. I begin dating Eddie Michael Black.

I thought he was handsome, tall, and sturdy. I was thirteen, and he was eighteen.

I was a virgin; Eddie and I dated for a year; I instantly fell in love. It was the best feeling ever; falling in love for the first time.

The first day, we met we had sex – I know it was too soon, but it was beautiful; the way he touched me.

I later learned that it was the worst day of my life. It's funny how one day could bring you so much happiness, yet so much pain!

Eddie eventually raped me repeatedly and beat me senseless. My life had become so miserable that I even attempted suicide. I wanted to die!

I had so many unanswered questions like; how could something so pure as love go so wrong? How did I get into this situation?

I thought we were in love; he had previously proposed to me and I accepted his proposal. I wanted a family!

However, Eddie becomes obsessive and abusive. I was not ready for that type of life.

I hate telling you this story, but maybe it would benefit you, and help you with your decision. The first time that Eddie raped me, it wounded me mentally.

The rape happened after we separated for six months. I was taking time away from our relationship and sex.

I was already trying to overcome past abuse. It was tragic – my life. Several times Eddie had beaten me beyond recognition.

When my family questioned what happened, I lied! I said that I had gotten into a fight with a classmate.

Well, the night of the rape; I was walking home in the snow. It was freezing outside, and although, I had on warm clothing; yet, I was still shivering.

I wore a black shirt, blue jeans, a long black coat that was buttoned up in the front, a red scarf covered my neck, black boots, and red mittens. I borrowed the clothing from one of my younger cousins; I couldn't afford anything at that age.

I was taking my usual midnight stroll across the lake, watching the stars, and talking to my parents in heaven. I guess, they could only do so much up there.

I knew no one here cared where I was, or what time I was coming home, and neither did I –care.

It was icy outside, and it seemed like it was getting even colder. It was darker than the norm because of the snow clouds.

I was walking across the frozen lake; puffs of white snow clouds were coming from my mouth as I breathe.

I heard loud footsteps trailing behind me – frightened by the sound, I kept looking back. I panicked, but I tried to stay calm. However, the heavy footsteps sounded as if the person was five feet away.

It was too dark; I could barely see my hands in front of me. I stopped, but I could still hear shoes tapping against the frozen lake. I begin walking faster and faster, nearly running.

I heard the footsteps chasing behind me and then I felt a hard nudge and I hit the ice. I landed flat on my belly; I thought I had broken a bone because the pain was very intense for a second. My mittens and clothing were sticking to the ice as I tried to get up.

Who's there? I yelled, frantically!

He said in a grave – deep tone, "Lester."

What do you want "Lester" I asked as my voice cracked? His voice sounded familiar; however, it was too dark to see his face.

"You – I want you! Every night, I watched you stroll down this path tempting me with your hot body. I come to see what you have to offer me."

Offer you? I started crying, and then I yelled out, "Sir, I do not know who you are. I have nothing to offer you. I am sure you have the wrong person. Please, let me go?

"Pamela Roosevelt, I am sure I have the right person. I am not stopping you from leaving. Am I?"

How do you know my name?

I heard – the sound of a belt buckle loosening. A piece of clothing fell to the ground next to me. I was so afraid; I was shaking.

I stretched my arm and felt the piece of clothing; it was a thick wool blanket; he leans down and begins spreading it across the ice. I could still hear the belt buckle dangling. I was too scared to move.

What are you doing?

"Getting what belongs to me."

What belongs to you?

"You will see."

I still could barely see him. He kept straightening out the blanket.

"Mum, why didn't you run?"

"Katherine, I was too afraid!"

Then "Lester" rolled me onto it, until I was lying flat on my back. Then he dropped his pants; I heard the belt buckle hit the ice. After all these years I could still hear that belt buckle clinking.

What are you doing? I asked.

"I told you that I am taking what belongs to me."

I begin crying; I was too afraid to scream. I was only thirteen; I don't even know if I fully understood what was going on.

Besides, I knew no one was coming; it was midnight, and everyone had gone to bed. I left the house once they had fallen asleep.

"Lester" lies on top of me and pulls down my pants and panties. He lifts my shirt up and removes my breasts from my bra. He is not the standard aggressive rapist.

He traces his tongue between my breasts down to my vagina and then licks and nibbles on my sweetness. He touches my entire vagina with his tongue.

"Mum?"

Let me finish, I want you to know it's not your fault, and you should not be ashamed of what that bastard done to you.

I screamed a prolonged moan as he begins to stroke faster. Aah, mmmmh, yesssss sssss baby!

Then I swallowed a sob and shouted No, No, Please No!

He grabs my thighs and stretched my legs apart. I kept crying and shaking.

He eases his erect penis inside of my vagina; slowly as if he was in love with me.

He places his wet mouth over my nipples and release my thighs. He wraps his thick arms around me and grips my unclothe back snugly as if he was a python.

His chest pressed against my breast. He leans down and sucks my nipples harder, biting and pulling on them with his sharp teeth. His' body rubs against mines as he strokes his penis in and out of my vagina.

I smell the scent of his body; it felt like Eddie. His touch seemed odd; he knew how to satisfy me sexually.

I wanted to be angry, but I desired to moan. Isn't that insane?

He places his finger against my clitoris. Then he rubs it softly as he strokes his penis inside of me.

Then he begins softly stroking in and out of my vagina as he softly kissed and sucked my firm nipples. The tip of his penis was slowly penetrating in and out of my vagina. Lester was teasing me and pleasing me at the same time.

"Eddie, is that you?" I asked as my breaths became heavier.

He begins moaning in pleasure, so he begins to relax, and his voice softens. I was not making love to him; however, I believe he felt as if he was making love to me. Since he kept repeating, "I love you!"

With each stroke, his breathing seemed to become naughtier as if he felt more and more pleasure. The strokes became more extended and softer – faster.

He was breathing more substantial and more massive. Then eventually, the strokes became harder and harder; I begin to yell!

Yass, damn; ooooh baby! STOP! STOP! Please get up – get off me; you are suffocating me! I was in heaven and hell at the same time.

Although, a small mental part of me enjoyed the rape! I knew it was wrong – I should not be enjoying this.

"You like it, I could tell. That's why you didn't stop me. You knew it was me, but you loved it. I could tell by your choked sobs. So, give it to me," Eddie said.

Get – up now, or I will scream louder, I yelled again – GET-UP.

My fear of him had left me once I became aware of who he was. I knew that all he could do is beat me, with his belt buckle to the face.

I felt that before – beaten by belts, fist, branches; it didn't matter whatever he grabbed. He hit me with it. I was immune to pain.

"Mum, how did you survive?"

Katherine, you learn how to endure!

Anyway, Eddie kept stroking inside of me until he released himself. He stayed on top of me with his penis still penetrated inside of me. I shoved him off me, pulled up my pants, and I ran as if my life depended on it.

However, I am not here to divulge my life story. I am here to get your attention, walk away, crawl away, but make sure you get out of that destructive relationship.

Katherine –

When I was twelve, my mother, Pamela Roosevelt, had given me some advice. I had all the ingredients that I needed to survive in life; I had the recipe; all I had to do is follow the instructions. They were simple, stay away from boys and relationships.

I recall my mother sitting me down beside her; she said, "Katherine Roosevelt, never stop dreaming, and never stop anticipating on them coming true."

"There will be times when you will malfunction; because life has a way of breaking you – humbling you. It might even wound you. You may hurt others as well. However, it's okay."

"Because life could be a challenge; however, life will not stop and let you fix your mistakes or comfort you. Time keeps ticking."

"So, you can choose to be the prey and failure or the achiever and a survivor of time. You can choose the stage you walk on or the ground you fall on."

"The phase that you may or may not go through, you can choose to rise above it or let it destroy you. But giving up is not a requirement; it's an option."

"You can be life's opponent or life's best friend. You have the key to it all and with the proper instructions to life – stardom nothing can hold you back. You are destined to become a legend."

My mother was my most prominent advocate, and I wanted that glory – that success. Since she did not discuss anything else, I supposed nothing else mattered.

Mother had given me all the advice that I needed to survive in this world, and she never mentioned love.

However, I ran into love despite the warnings! Then I hit rock bottom unexpectedly – not financially, however emotionally. Here is where my story begins.

CHAPTER *2*

K atherine –

I was on my boss' bed; with my face turned towards the head-board. My eyes were blackened; a large knot was on my forehead. I am sure I had a few wounds.

My face drenched in blood, from the cuts under my eyes. More bruises covered my body, and love bites.

I couldn't allow my mother to see me like this – bruised and disgusted. Then she and father walked into Jason's bedroom.

Mother took a step back; I thought she was going to pass out. She stood paralyzed to that spot. Mother closed her painful eyes, tears fell.

"Who the hell did this," my father asked with a piercing stare? He was in a rage.

I was afraid to tell him that it was Thomas. Because a tiny part of me still cared for him. I did not want his image or his reputation damaged.

My parents began questioning me; I attempted to answer; however, my lips were pressing against one another. Jason uttered Thomas' name and it broke a piece of my heart.

Jason revealed one of my top-secrets that I had hidden for months. My life was filled with hush-hushed conversations and then suddenly everything is becoming public. I was ashamed.

My father wanted to kill Thomas; however, I begged him not

to, and then I made him promise not to say one word. Unrestricted to speak, father bolted out the room in rage.

However, mother stopped him. She grabbed his arm, "Let it go, Paul," she said.

◆ ◆ ◆

The biggest fight between Thomas and I started at the Christmas party. However, there were plenty more.

The winter of 2010, Taylor's Northeastern Oil & Gas Corporation had their first Christmas party. We were thrilled! The women went shopping for long elegant dresses, and the men shopped for stylish, sleek tuxedos.

I went to Dee-Cee's Salon & Spa in preparation for the party. I got my hair, make-up, and nails done. After the stylist finished, I turned around to see myself.

I touched the mirror to see if it was, indeed, my image. Who was this beautiful woman? For a brief second, my pain disappeared, and I discovered myself once again. I had lost myself a long time ago.

My hair dangled and swung against my shoulders and neck. My skin was golden and smooth. The ruby red lipstick made my lips look enticing and velvety. The sparkling gold eyeshadow flattered my gorgeous eyebrows and lashes as I batted them. I looked stunning!

However, I was not quite finished pampering myself, not yet. I went to the best boutique in town to buy the sexiest dress that I could find, which complemented my body. I took off my business suit for a gorgeous evening gown and a night of excitement.

I found the precise dress; it was seamless and just right for the occasion. Thomas had stumbled upon the invitation several days before the party and insisted on being my guest.

I was a little disappointed because I knew he would do all he could to prevent me from enjoying the social event, and although I felt unnerved, I did not allow him to stop me.

I was ready to stagger Jason with my beauty., impress him, then sneak away his heart. Nonetheless, knock him to his knees with my loveliness, and make him beg me for kisses.

It was snowing outside, and Thomas and I had driven to the party separately. Thomas arrived in his Rolls-Royce thirty minutes ahead of me. The gathering was at a venue in Washington D.C.; the site decorated with Christmas trees, poinsettia plants, dozens and dozens of Christmas roses, golden candles all different sizes with robins tied around them, and rosebuds placed in the center of each table.

Crystal teardrop chandeliers, mitoses, and Christmas lights were hanging from the ceiling; it was awesome. I took a second to walk around; it was terrific.

The aroma of apple cinnamon pies, sugar cookies, jasmine plants, and pine trees was in the air.

Thomas was sipping on a glass of champagne and socializing with the crowd until I walked through the door. I knew I captivated the group; there was a moment of silence as I walked into the room. I took off my fur coat and revealed my mouthwatering curves.

Thomas and Jason needed a handkerchief to clean up the dribble. I stood tall in my gold stilettos. My dress was strapless with gold transparent interior and red lace exterior.

Underneath the dress, I had on red lace panties and a bra. The gold almost blended in perfectly with my skin; I appeared to be naked underneath the lace.

The dress clung to my size twelve body perfectly as I waltzed around the venue. By the way the men were staring, I believe I tempted most of them with my sex appeal.

Romantic music was playing loudly. I danced around with Thomas; however, it was challenging to follow.

Thomas was pulling me like a puppet, forcing me to keep up with him. The floor felt like a skating rink. My shoes kept slipping off as he jerked my stiff body around. I felt emotionless as we danced.

However, I smiled and danced anyway. Jason was handsome

in his black tuxedo, white dress shirt, French cufflinks, red tie, and a pair of black shiny dress shoes.

I had to use that same handkerchief he used to wipe my drips. My eyes were delighted when I saw the sexy man of my dreams standing in front of me. He looked lip-smacking good, and he had pleasant manners.

Was he the answer to my request? I wanted to be free, and someone sent me an extraordinary man wrapped in a big gold bow with a note that said, "It's just for you, Katherine."

When I looked into Jason's eyes, I could tell he had erupted with rage; my red dress had him scorching with envy, and his stares showed it. I desperately wanted to be in his loving arms more than ever.

His stares fascinated me; his jealousy turned into a charm. His desperation was luring me. I was cleverly hoping and expecting him to ask me for a dance; I was set to say, yes.

Exactly – the same thing that I hated most about Thomas, I admired about Jason. Maybe it was the way I found myself yearning for love, and protection, which caused me to overlook Jason's flaws.

I pretended not to be interested in Jason, however, I was lying to myself. I ached for his attention.

I felt the presence of someone standing close behind me. My impulse was to turn around right away, however I knew it was Jason.

It seemed as if I had smelled the fragrance of his cologne a thousand times; it had become familiar. I kept looking forward.

I took a small step frontward to tease him, and so did he. His body brushed against mines.

Oh! — I sighed softly. Then he leaned forward; his lips grazed my ear, and he softly whispered, "You look beautiful! May I have this dance?

Yes, yes, yes, and yes, what took you so long to ask? I thought to myself.

Jason's deep voice sent chills down my back as he breathes against my ear; it was Déjà vu – prom night all over again.

I cracked my mouth to say yes, however nothing came out. He asked me again. Ahem! I cleared my throat, and said "Yes,"

I turned around, but he was standing too close. My lips brushed against his'. He looked deep into my eyes; they were sparkling and filled with love. His stare was seeping into my heart, and his eyes were mocking mines.

Jason laid his hands on my waist, and I put my arms around his neck. We embraced each other tightly.

My frail body was under his control. I pressed my head against his chest. I heard his' heart beating fast, and so was mine.

Anxiously—

Thomas sprinted across the floor. When I saw him rushing towards me, I knew it would be trouble, but I was not ready to let Jason go, not yet.

Seeing Jason again sparked a flame in me that a fire extinguisher could not put out. I still felt a tenderness for him, and it was extraordinary.

Thomas gripped my arm tightly; "You are hurting me." I said. Then he snatched me away from Jason. However, led by a more deep-rooted passion for Jason, I pulled away from Thomas. Then I continued to dance.

Jason slid left, so did I, and when he drifted right, I followed. Jason's hands were on the lower part of my back, with my hands wrapped around his neck.

Jason turned me in circles fluidly; our feet went from side to side. We were amateur dancers driven by passion.

I could see the anger on Thomas' face. However, my passion for Jason was persuading my heart. We continued dancing slowly with the music. Jason turned my body around until he stood behind me.

I moved my hips against the lower part of his body. The dimmed lights made us focus less on the things that were around us.

Jason turned me around again, and my face pressed against

his. My breast thrust against his chest.

Oh! I whispered. Jason was grinding his erected penis against me, and it affected me. I was thinking about sexual things that I had never imagined doing to any man.

Thomas never aroused me or stirred up such passion before. I sought to please Jason in ways that no other woman could, and my desire for him was blazing out of control.

I started to cry while we were dancing. I know Jason thought I was crazy, but I finally felt free, and the spot-on song came on expressing exactly how I felt.

"Chandelier" by Sia,…"I'm gonna swing from the chandelier…, I'm gonna live like tomorrow doesn't exist…, Cause I'm just holding on for tonight."

We danced, and we danced; it was quite seductive. I was still crying. The song ended, but my mind was still dancing.

I was not ready for the party to end. Jason wiped my tears, but they were more in-depth than the water that he wiped from my face.

After we finished dancing, he thanked me and kissed me on the cheek. Everything about Jason delighted me. I walked away, but I left a part of my heart with him.

Thomas stood there with anger in his eyes, but he could not make a big scene and ruin his outstanding reputation. Nor could he stop me from dancing.

Jason and I danced again and again. I felt the large lump in his pants pressing against me. However, I ignored it and kept dancing.

Thomas walked away, but he watched me, and he stared into my eyes as he exited the venue.

However, Jason and I were still dancing; it was endless. Jason held me in his arms like a delicate rose.

His muscular body held me up as I leaned against him. He gripped me tightly as I watched Thomas walk away.

Ah! —

I fell in love with Jason over and over again, and I was willing to suffer the outcome for that beam of love. I was experiencing it, that happiness.

I felt complete when Jason held me. For a second, it felt like this was the end of our love story. However, it had just begun.

Jason had a secured spot in my heart since the night of the prom, I could not stop thinking about him. Thomas held me, hostage, physically, but Jason had captured my emotions. I was living for the moment.

Jason —

I was dazed and allured by Katherine's charisma. I stood against the wall and glowered at her; she returned the glares. Despite the large crowd, she was the only woman who possessed my heart, and I desired to sweep her off her feet.

That night I had fallen in love with Katherine's beauty; she had already wowed me with her cleverness. However, words could not describe what I felt.

I was speaking with the secretary, but I could barely concentrate on the conversation. My eyes stayed on Katherine. I despised Thomas touching her. I wanted her to myself more than ever.

Thomas stepped away briefly to get another glass of champagne. I spotted an opportunity to dance with Katherine; however, she was mingling with the other employees at the time.

Soft romantic music was playing, and the lights were dim. It was a romantic moment. I went over; I said excuse me, ladies, as I clutched Katherine's hand tightly and then led her to the dance floor. We held each other closely and glided across the floor.

Our hearts connected as we danced like always. "What are you doing to me?" I asked. The pressure was rising between my thighs more and more. Katherine aroused me, under the influenced of her body, my penis rose.

The way she moved; I could feel the heat coming from her red dress as if it was on fire. I met countless women, but no one had ever made me feel so feeble. I was fascinated.

After we finished dancing, I thanked her and kissed her on the cheek. The dance mesmerized me; I looked down and noticed the lump in my pants had gotten even more abundant.

Katherine had touched more than my heart. Thomas gripped Katherine by her arm firmly and snatched her away from me.

But Katherine pulled away from him and continued to dance. I loved her even more. At that moment, I knew that nothing could come between us, and she was my destiny.

Thomas –

I walked away, and then I saw her boss, Jason going towards Katherine. Before I could get back to her, they were already dancing.

Jason was standing in front of Katherine, dancing as if they were in love. It felt as if a knife pierced my heart.

He turned Katherine around in circles; she laughed with her head tilted back. Her smile was huger than the one she had when we first met. She was wrapped in Jason's arm, holding onto him.

They seemed like they were dancing on air and I was fuming! I went up to her face to face. Jason was looking at me as though he wanted to fight me, and I was ready. I grabbed Katherine by her arm, and she pulled away from me.

I guess her passion for Jason led her; I was surprised when she showed so much courage. I kept watching her dance in another man's arms.

I held my rage inside, but I wanted to stretch my arm back as far as I could, then swing forward and slap her to the floor.

My rage was controlling me, and it was out of control. I was obsessed with Katherine, and I had reached my limit. I could not watch them any longer. I left, but I looked at Katherine as I walked away.

I punched the palm of my hand with my fist, and at that point, my rage had reached its limit. I did not care who saw me.

My anger was uncontrollable. When I arrived home, I was

standing outside in the snow, impatiently waiting and grinding my teeth. The snowflakes were not cooling me down.

Katherine pulled up in the driveway. When she got close to me, I rushed towards her. I grabbed her by the hair and yanked it – then kissed her on the lips.

I dragged her inside the house by her hair. I went to the bathroom and turned the cold water on; I needed to cool her off.

I wanted to do things to her that I may regret later, but right now, I was going to enjoy doing them. I was going to do what was best for our relationship, but Katherine did not understand that.

Why was that so hard for Katherine to understand? I'm doing what is best for us.

Katherine –

On my way home, I exited to the side of the road to gather my thoughts. I had to remember my responsibilities.

I had to pull myself together. I opened the door, got out of the car, and walked down the path next to the building; it was dark and cold, and the snow-covered the ground.

My footprints trailed behind me, and so did my soul. I had on a long fur coat, but I was not afraid of the thieves. Once a man deprives you of your self-esteem, there was nothing more to be afraid of or worth keeping – you lose value.

I was trying to understand where I belong and what would be my next move? Positively not Thomas, I hated him as much as I cared for him.

However, what was sadder is that I was more afraid of being lonely than being hit by Thomas. The truth is, dozens of people surrounded me, but no one recognized my distress or cared about my tears or depression.

I guess that qualifies me as being alone. I had to get home; I got back into the car and drove off.

As I drove down the driveway, I quivered. I was sitting in the vehicle with the window down, too terrified to get out.

Shelley Jenkins

Then in an assertive tone, Thomas yelled, "Are you hot for Jason?" I had to retain my tongue; I could not answer the question truthfully. I was steaming with desire for him, and I wanted to rip his clothes off. I wanted to make love for the first time to Jason.

Jason had secured a spot in my heart and my bedroom. My feelings were so intense that I managed to forget my pain. The emotions I had for Jason were not just temporary; they were permanent. I was in love with him!

That night, Thomas was lustful, his tongue licked my skin; it felt creepy and wet. He must have been drinking while he was waiting for me; I smelled a strong scent of liquor. I choked from the smell.

Thomas snatched me from the car and then dragged me to the bathtub. My skin scraped and bled. I screamed and begged, "Pl-Pleeease, Pleeease, Pleeease, and Please No!" – Thomas ripped my clothes off and forced me into the tub.

I never had sex before, and I did not want my first encounter to be like this. Thomas told me that love was for fools.

I guess I am a fool. I was saving my body for my husband-to-be and my first love, Jason, and now that was not possible.

Tonight, I had just returned home from dancing with Jason. Now, Thomas is raping me as if I was shabby and worthless. I began fighting pushing, screaming, and kicking him.

However, he trapped me under him. I could not stop crying, pleeease no, you have no right to touch me. "NO! —Pleeease, No," I kept screaming. I was hoping someone heard my desperate cry.

However, Thomas continued to rape me and hit me. His tantrums were getting worse. No matter how loud I screamed, no one came to my rescue, and Thomas enjoyed seeing me frail.

Thomas punched me in the face, and he hit me until I became numb. I was too weak to fight anymore. Blood seeped into the bathtub.

I felt worthless! I sobbed until I could not cry anymore. I closed my eyes; so, I could not see him, but I sensed the stink

28

of his spicy cologne and sweat. My heart was pumping, and the beats were increasing rapidly. [Dup – dup, dup, dup - dup]

Thomas' strokes became more forceful and harsher; I scratched him, but it did not stop him. I wanted to kill myself while he was screwing me. Then he released his seed inside of me.

I was bleeding slightly from the tear. I was sobbing uncontrollably. Thomas said, "You wanted it, and I gave it to you." How could he?

"No," I groaned one last time. I was heartbroken, ashamed, and angry with myself.

An intelligent woman, yet I did not see the signs. Thomas was hyper-aggressive.

Maybe I just ignored the warnings. Thomas got up, and glowingly walked away. I lay helpless and stripped of my dignity.

I wondered! — I wept; if Jason knew the truth, would he still want me? Could Jason continue to love me? If so, how could he, when I hated myself.

I felt filthy, no matter how hard I scrubbed my body, the water could not remove those feelings, and the soap could not clean me, or take the warmth of his skin from underneath my fingernails.

Maybe if I refilled the tub with clean water, I could wash the dirt off, but I felt the same no matter how many times I refilled the bathtub and no matter how many times I bathed.

I lay in the water with my face down; I took a deep breath and breathed out and retook a deep breath. I coughed as I choked on the sudsy water.

Then I placed my head under the water again and held it there for as long as I could. After several minutes, I came back up coughing and gasping for air.

CHAPTER 3

K atherine –

I wanted to punish Thomas by stripping away his control. I was an emotional wreck because of him, and this was not my first suicide attempt, I thought about it numerous of times. I went to my doctor; she prescribed medication to help me with the nightmares.

Thomas ruined my happiness and the perfect world I savored; I was devastated. Thomas's love had become an obsession, and his addiction for me was destroying our relationship, razing my sanity.

I wanted to die, but my desire for Jason kept stopping me. I could not kill myself. I have asked myself a million times. "How could I go from sailing on top of the clouds to gasping for air underneath the water?" My mother did not prepare me for this.

Thomas was hurting me daily – physically and emotionally. Love doesn't hurt. Well, the pain that Thomas inflicted on me was excruciating.

However, the rape had pushed me to the edge. Thomas had hit me before, and my body may have become immune to it.

However, to steal my purity – my virginity that I was saving for my husband was intolerable; I was exhausted, and I needed to rest. However, I kept wondering, who would want me, a pathetic rape victim?

I was vulnerable; scars covered me inside and out. "Lord, help me!" I cried out. Work was the only place where I felt safe, and it was the most secure place.

However, Thomas did not like me working. Jason would ask me to stay a few extra hours; I made excuses for why I couldn't wait. I wouldn't survive another slap or kick.

I couldn't tell Jason the truth. I was a grown woman with a curfew. What would he think? How could I be so weak? He wouldn't understand my fear.

Where was my knight with the shining armor, my hero – my prince charming? Where was my father? I needed someone to rescue me, and I needed someone to fight my battles since I didn't have the strength.

Sometimes I stared in the mirror to see who I had become. What happened to that motivated woman? What happened to my aspirations?

Thomas took everything from me. I felt like an abused kid who couldn't do anything right. However, I never shared my life story with anyone.

Would they judge me for the poor decisions that I have made? Yes, I had a great family who believed in doing the right thing.

Well, after so many slaps, I lost my vision of what was right. I couldn't think logically. However, my mother nearly discovered the truth.

There was this one incident; I was sitting on my bed. Thomas had come home and accused me of cheating.

I denied it because, at the time, I wasn't. I told Thomas that it was he that was cheating. He became angry, and he slapped me!

Thomas did not believe me when I said I wasn't cheating. He grabbed me by the hair, and then he slangs me to the floor. Then he pinned my hands and feet behind my back, and he started slapping and punching me from behind. I cried not only that day, but every day.

My mother had come over unexpectedly; I had to halt the tears – I had to be "strong." I was in the bathroom crying and rushing to put on makeup before she saw me.

I finished just in time. I had forgotten to lock the door. Mother walked in, and my face dropped to the floor.

I was taking prescribed medication. My eyes were bloodshot.

"Baby, what's wrong? Why were you crying?" She hugged me.

I grunted, "I wasn't, was I?"

"Are you in pain?"

I shook my head, No!

"Stop it...do not lie to me, Katherine! I never recall you having any, health issues and I heard you grunt. Are you okay?"

Yes, mother, I am okay!

"Why are you taking those pills – what are they for – how long have you been taking them?"

I began screaming, with my hands lifted into the air. Mother, I am under a lot of stress, there are projects due, and the pills help me to be less worrisome. So, stop questioning me. Please?

"Katherine Roosevelt, what is going on with you? You know that you can come to your father or me if you have any issues."

I sighed. "Yes, Mother! Please do not tell Dad!

"You know we don't keep secrets, but I will keep your skeletons buried just for a little while."

Thanks, Mum! I assure you that you never have to worry about me. I have a massive project due immediately, so there is a lot of pressure on me. I was taking the pills to relieve the stress."

"Okay..."

I could tell she wasn't satisfied with my answer, nor did she believe me. Nevertheless, she knew I was not ready to discuss what was genuinely bothering me.

My heart started beating faster as we exited the bathroom. I was concerned that my mother would tell my father what was going on.

I did not want the only man who unquestionably made me feel valuable to regret calling me his daughter — what a mess my life had become.

If I was such a smart person, why was I in this predicament? I kept asking myself the same questions.

Because I couldn't forgive me; I had broken my promise to my parents. My last words were, I will make you proud.

I wondered how proud they would be, besides the pain was becoming harder to cope with; it never became more pleasant. I kept waiting for a brighter day.

Before Thomas came into my life, I was happy, but now each day seems to be a struggle to smile. The pain medication and Jason were the only two things that began relieving some of my aches and kept me sane.

I grieved every single day. Trying to keep my abusive life a secret was more than I could sustain. I was ready to stop my life; it seemed much, much more comfortable.

However, I couldn't confess to my mother that I was taking more pain medication than recommended because I wanted to overdose. Alternatively, I wore long sleeves to veil the cut marks.

I couldn't tell her how many times I held my head underwater because I was practicing for the audition of death. I could not tell her how many times I drove across a bridge during the wee hours of the night, tempted to roll off it.

I wanted to confess, but how would that make her feel? How would people look at me, like the ugly person that I am?

After my mother left, I lay on the sofa in the living room and fell asleep. I heard Thomas yelling from the bedroom. "KATHERINE, where are you?" I jumped, he frightened me!

Spontaneously, I lay my head on the pillow, and then I pretended to be asleep. I heard the squeaky bedroom door open and Thomas' bare feet as they slapped against the wooden floor. Then he lifted me from the sofa and carried me back into the bedroom.

I was terrified; I didn't want him to rape me again. I never questioned him or opened my eyes.

Lying beside him was the longest night ever. I tossed, and I turned; I could not sleep. Teardrops fell on the pillow.

When I thought that I was safe, I felt him pulling down my pajama pants, and he pulled down his'. He shoved his penis inside of my vagina, and he started beating inside of me with his long hard penis.

Tears flooding down my face, I'm praying to God, please help me. But, first, I had to help myself.

My parents had told me that God was not a forceful God, but I wished he had forced the empathy that I felt from Thomas straight out of my heart.

After Thomas finished, he rolled off me and then he fell asleep. He was snoring with his arms wrapped around my waist. How could he sleep so peacefully after what he had done?

I wanted to grab something and start beating him until my pain was gone, but I would be the same animal as I envision him to be.

Finally, I fell asleep! —

I dreamed that I was in a different world with tall buildings that surrounded me. Jason held a large shield in one hand, and a sword in the other hand, and he stood in front of me. The structures represented strength, and Jason was my guard, just as my father protected his fortress.

CHAPTER 4

T he next day, I woke up, and the wounds were still there. I wore extra makeup to work to conceal my black eye and bruises.

I walked into my dark office and turned the lights on. My big bug-eyes blinked quickly; I was surprised when I saw Jason sitting in my chair with breakfast on my desk.

Regardless of how depressed I felt, I could not resist beaming when I saw him. I pushed the breakfast to the side, sat on the desktop, and then crossed my legs.

Jason gazed into my eyes, but I dropped my head. I could feel my emotions boiling up again. He laid his head against my leg and kissed my knee.

Then he slid my skirt up and began kissing and licking my inner thigh. Then up to my lace panties. He used his tongue muscles to slide them over. His wet, warm stiff tongue massages my vagina.

My heart started beating faster – harder than ever, and I felt a soft pulse between my thighs. Jason's touch was different from Thomas'; it was pleasant.

Then my desk phone began to ring. I recognized the telephone number on the caller ID device. "It is from Thomas."

"Damn," we both said! I didn't want Jason to stop and by Jason's response either did he.

Jason licked his lips and stood up; he kicked the desk and walked away. I waited for a second, and then I answered the phone.

Thomas immediately began apologizing! He said he didn't understand why he lost control. Nevertheless, he did not want another man touching me; he asked, "Please forgive me."

I remembered begging him, "Please stop," but he had no compassion for me. So, why should I pity him?

I did not say a word; I just listened to the blah, blah, and blah, blah. Thomas shouted, "Do you hear me talking to you?"

Yes! I mumbled.

"Do you forgive me?" He said in an aggressive tone.

I [pause] I [pause] I –

"Speak up and answer the question."

I could not answer that question truthfully, but then I barely whispered, Yes. Even though I was afraid, and I told Thomas yes, in my heart, I refused to accept his apology.

"Speak up and stop whispering!" He demanded. However, before I could answer the question louder, he replied, "We will talk after work."

Those words always concerned me, and I began to panic! What does that mean? What was going to happen? I asked Thomas.

However, Thomas slammed the phone down in my ear. Jason asked "Are you okay?

Yes!

"What did he say?"

Nothing!

"Why were you so afraid?"

I wasn't!

"Yes, you were! Is he hitting you?

NO!

"Are you sure because that will not be tolerated."

I SAID he is not hitting me!

"Okay!"

I needed to break free from Thomas' emotional and physical restraints. I was searching for a way out, and by the sound of Jason voice; he was offering it.

I was willing to take it. However, I needed more time. I

couldn't just walk away; Thomas wouldn't allow that.

It was five o'clock and time for me to get off. However, I wasn't in a rush to leave; I felt protected at work.

Thomas didn't reside with me, but he had a key to my home; he came and went as he pleased. I had no control over my life.

I couldn't challenge him; I knew Thomas would never allow me to leave – at least not alive. Later that night, I went home, ate dinner, and showered; as I lay on my bed, I fell asleep, and I had another dream.

However, this dream was passionate! —

I was clothed entirely and cuddled in Jason's muscular, nude arms. Lying next to his bare chest; it was mind-blowing.

We softly kissed; my lips partly opened, so was his'. We kissed passionately; it was the sweetest taste ever.

Jason slid his tongue gently down my neck; he began licking me as if I was gooey melted chocolate. My body jerked, the sensation was so inflamed, so real that it waked me from my sleep. Jason's innocent touch made me feel pure again.

I couldn't sleep; I continued to lie across the bed, imagining that I shared all my murkiest secrets with Jason. Then I got up and took another shower before Thomas came home.

The water ran down my body; I imagined Jason standing behind me, kissing and licking my back, holding me tightly and assuring me that everything would be okay.

Then I heard loud footsteps speeding toward the bathroom. I quickly turned off the water and rushed out of the shower before Thomas forced himself to join me.

I was drying my legs with the towel, and then the door opened. The tension between us was powerful enough to slam the door back closed.

He asked me why I was bathing so late. I could not believe I had to answer such a silly question. But I told him, I just woke up, I was tired from work. I lay down to take a nap, and I overslept."

"Let us eat dinner," he said and then closed the door. I went into my bedroom, found a thick winter pajama set, and then put it on. I fixed dinner; we ate. Then he said. It's time for dessert," I knew what that meant.

I pulled down my pants; anger was boiling inside. I lay on the kitchen floor. My entire body was blank.

I had become immune to rape. I couldn't even cry anymore.

After Thomas finished, we went to bed. I was hoping that he was too tired to force himself on me again.

When he finished, it was the same repeated line "Can you forgive me." But after all the hurt that he caused me, I would never forgive him. He would not have that power over me ever again.

He apologized again and again. However, I heard the same lies before over and over, "I'm sorry." Thomas held me in his revolting arms all night as though nothing ever happened.

CHAPTER 5

K atherine –

I recall the first year of high school; it was the most crucial chapter of my life – the core that's why I had no time for love. I had led by example, most of my teen life.

I started admiring myself, and I based everything on how I felt, what I thought, and where I was going, which was an essential part of my life. I began to form the foundation to my stardom, which started with me.

I was excelling in life. There were no limitations. "The sky was the limit," that is what my mother told me. Well, I was drifting on a cloud, reaching beyond the sky; "trying to find that glory."

I had built a pedestal, which stood as tall as my ego and as high as a collegiate peak. I was skillful, and the most intelligent student at the school and I knew it.

Arrogance had swollen my head. I was prepared to astound the world, and I was well equipped to do so.

An intelligent woman such as me could overcome any situation. At least that is what I assumed!

◆ ◆ ◆

However, Katherine had met Thomas while she was in college; it was her last year and a half. She had become lonely and a little desperate for attention.

Adult life seemed to be a lot different than high school; she wanted a man. However, the one whom she desired had abandoned her.

She called Maryann every single day; she saw Katie and her family daily. However, she needed something more.

It was the last summer before graduation; Katherine asked Maryann and Katie to come and visit her. They agreed to stay with Katherine for a week.

She missed them so much, especially Jason! MaryAnn caught the first plane to Washington D. C.

Katie resided locally in their hometown; she came straight over. Then Kathrine and Katie went to the airport to pick up MaryAnn. They were excited to see one another.

Katherine and Katie kissed and hugged MaryAnn, and the ladies complimented each other. Then they got in the car and left. Katherine asked Katie if she had heard from Jason. Katie nodded, "Yes."

"Katie, did he ask about me?"

"He has been swamped! He's working hard and going to school; I hardly ever see him anymore."

"HAS he asked for me," Katherine asked in a firm tone.

"No, Katherine, I'm sorry!"

Katherine begins to cry, "I lost him forever," she said. Katie empathized with her, but she could not take away her pain. Katie could only try to comfort her while she was grieving.

August 2008,

The ladies were sitting down on the sofa in the living room talking about Jason. Then someone knocked on the door.

Katherine asked, "Who is it?"

"Sandy."

Katherine opened the door and then asked Sandy to have a

seat.

"No, thank you, I am not staying." Sandy said. "I stopped by to invite you to a birthday party; it starts at 9:00 pm."

"Maryann and Katie, would you like to go?" Katherine asked?

"Yes!" they said in unison.

While Sandy was walking away, she said, "Dress casual."

Katherine arrived at the party around 10:30 pm. She wore a pair of skin-tight white jeans and a lace blue blouse. They found a table away from the big crowd.

The girls were sitting around the table drinking and giggling. Sandy saw Katherine seated across the room; Katherine's head tipped back; she was laughing and smiling for the first time.

Sandy told Mindy and Thomas, "Excuse me, I see a friend, and I need to say hello."

Sandy walked towards the table where Katherine and her friends were sitting. She walked up to Katherine.

Katherine stood up, then Sandy kissed Katherine on the cheek. "Glad you came!" Sandy said.

"I will be leaving soon but thank you for inviting me."

"Don't forget to grab a drink; snatch one of these single guys."

The women laughed! "I'm going to mingle with the crowd," Sandy said as she danced away.

Thomas turned his head, snooping. He was curious to see whom Sandy meeting was with.

The only woman Thomas noticed was Katherine. The tall, handsome, good-looking young man came up to Katherine and introduced himself as soon as Sandy left the table.

Thomas –

I thought, Wow! That was the first word that came to my mind! I was standing around at a party associating with my friends when I glanced up and saw a young woman with golden-colored skin, smiling and chatting at the table with two other women.

She had a peaceful and perfect white smile; her hair was

black, long, and straight. Her eyes were as beautiful as a brown diamond.

I felt a deep attraction blooming inside of me. My attention was drawn to Katherine the entire evening.

I know love, at first sight, is so cliché, but that is how I felt. I walked up to her and then introduced myself. She smiled and stood up. She said her name was Katherine. I am in love with you, Katherine, I thought to myself.

Katherine's blouse was tight against the curves of her body. I could see through the lace blouse; her beautiful breasts were peeping above the top.

Her nipples were large and stiff and poking out. I could not stop staring at her bare skin through the lace blouse. What I was really in love with was her body. I wanted it!

After staring at her chest for about thirty seconds, I hesitated for several long seconds, and then I said, "Nice to meet you two." Katherine's friends giggled; "I apologized! It's nice to meet you."

Mindy stood up to watch us; about ten minutes into the conversation, I left the table.

"So, who is she?" Mindy asked.

Mindy – I don't know, she said her name was Katherine. I was speaking to her and her friends; I will walk her to her car later. No worries baby, I love you!

"No worries, huh? Okay, and I love you too?"

I kissed Mindy on the cheek. However, she knew that I enjoyed spreading my love. I have been with Mindy for years, and been with dozens of women before, she's not going anywhere.

I planned on chasing Katherine's skirt right off her. I wanted to taste that vagina; by the looks of her body, I knew it was good.

When the party was over, I walked up to Katherine and then walked her outside to her car. I kissed her goodnight on the cheek.

Short story, Katherine and I began dating a couple of weeks later. I was falling in love with her quicker than I intended. Maybe it was because she told me that she had only kissed one man, which was intriguing.

Perhaps I could take his spot and kiss those big nipples. I wanted her all to myself.

Katie –

Katherine lured by loneness; she was too blind to see he was not the man for her. He was not even her type of man. "My name is Thomas Kilpatrick." He said as he hesitated for a second; he was staring at her blouse; her firm nipples were poking against the shirt. Katherine said, "Nice to meet you."

Thomas did not know the truth; the possibility of Katherine giving another man a chance at love was nearly impossible. She loved Jason, but they had broken up.

However, when you are lonely, you make hasty decisions. Katherine reached out her hand and then said to Thomas, "I am Katherine Roosevelt.

Katherine –

Thomas briefly sat at the table next to me, but not for long. He appeared to be in a rush; ten minutes into our conversation, he stood up.

"I'll see you around,"

Okay!

I turned to Maryann and Katie. That was a little odd, the way he walked away, I said to them.

"He's a bit strange." Katie said.

"I don't like him," Maryann said.

However, I ignored them. Finding a man was another check-mark off my list of to do's.

Maryann added, "He seems full of himself, and he's way too serious. I do not know if he's the one for you."

MaryAnn, you and I thought Jason was the one, but look at us and where is Jason? He promised – 'I would be here forever,' and again, where is he?

"You pushed him away," said Katie. Well, I will not lose an opportunity to be with a man who is interested in me for 'Give it time.' It's been three years since high school; how much time does he need?

Maryann said, "You are making a mistake, but – it is your life and your choice." Thomas came back to the table; he walked me to the car.

Maryann and Katie walked behind us; Maryann stood by the car door; she stared vacantly with hatred in her eyes. She truly disliked Thomas, and she warned me repeatedly that he was egotistic, and something just wasn't right about him.

However, I thought he was cute, and I was searching for a man to replace the feelings that I had for Jason.

I had taken Maryann and Katie's feelings into consideration, but I had to do what was right for me. Several days after the party, Maryann and Katie returned home.

Thomas and I began dating. We did not see each other often, but it did not matter because the emphasis was on my school grades.

It was a pricey relationship. However, Thomas didn't interfere with my education, and I did not snoop into his engagements.

But that was not the core of the expenses. There was a more profound penalty to pay for love.

Katie –

After a few weeks, Katherine called Maryann and I on the three-way to share the incredible news that she was dating Thomas. Maryann and I were silent; Katherine had given another man a chance to be with her?

It was unlike Katherine to date anyone so quickly. It took her months to say "Hello" to Jason. However, she was dating Thomas within two to three weeks. Something wasn't right.

CHAPTER 6

Thomas was interning at a reputable law firm. Katherine was impressed, a law-abiding man that was interested in her!

Yes, Thomas had a firm attitude. However, Katherine had a thing for hard men, and she enjoyed the attention.

On their first date, Katherine told Thomas, "I have only kissed one man before and he was my high school crush." However, she never mentioned Jason's name.

Thomas was angry, but it was too soon to react; he had recently started dating Katherine. He did not want to hear anything about another man; he was the jealous type.

Many men tried to befriend Katherine, but Thomas warned each of them personally, that "a new sheriff was in town," and he had placed his star right above Katherine's heart.

Thomas –

Immediately, I begin thinking that Katherine belonged to me. She was my leading lady. However, I was dating Mindy, but there was something about Katherine that overcame me.

Katherine called my phone, and I answered right away, I never missed any of her phone calls or wanted anything other than Katherine's love. I enjoyed hearing her soft voice.

Everything stopped when she was around; she was the most important person in my life; every day felt like our first-day meeting.

My emotions were growing, and they were getting stronger

and stronger by the second. When we were separated, I grieved.

I had dozens of pictures of her in my photo album. When we were apart, it felt as if she was still close to me, especially when I rubbed her face and kissed her.

Although it was just an image of her, it felt as good as being next to her. I was in a relationship, but I needed to know where Katherine was at all the time.

She belonged to me, and when I didn't get my way, I forced it upon her. I didn't allow her to speak with men or look at them.

Katherine needed my permission for everything. If her family and friends only knew that Katherine was calling me for my approval before she even went out with them; they would be concerned.

I watched her every move, and when she turned, even if I was there by coincidence, I was there. At least that's what I told her; it was by accident.

I stalked Katherine, and she was afraid of me; it did not matter if I wasn't there; she was too petrified to disobey me. It was like my eyes were on her all the time.

Control –

Katherine believed that Thomas was in love with the fact that she was a virgin, and that flattered her. However, Thomas hid his harmful intentions from her!

Thomas eventually graduated from college and became a well-known attorney commended for his toughness inside and outside of the courtroom. He was a wealthy man with a lot of power and the ability to manipulate any situation, even with Katherine.

For instance, there was October 5, 2009—a Monday afternoon. It was Thomas and Katherine's first dinner date. They were at the restaurant; the male waiter turned toward Katherine to take her order [ladies first]. Thomas interrupted the waiter.

"There is no reason for you to speak with Katherine, I'll place her order."

"Thomas, you are rude?"

"What would you like?"

Katherine looks at the waiter, then she says, "I would like – shrimp, creamy pasta, and a glass of white wine."

"Whore listen."

The server said, "I'll be back."

"I am sorry – I am so sorry, Katherine, I didn't mean that?"

The server served a few other customers, and then returned to the table. He turned towards Katherine again [ladies first].

"Are you ready, ma'am?"

"Yes!"

"Sir, didn't I ask you – not to speak with her?"

"Thomas, you are being rude."

"It's okay ma'am!" The server turned towards Thomas. "What would you like?"

"Nothing and get me another waiter."

"What is wrong with you?" Katherine asked. Her eyes locked on Thomas, and she crossed her arms.

"Get away from this table and get me another server NOW," Thomas yelled.

Right then Katherine should have run away as fast as she could, but she stayed. When the server left the table, Thomas began yelling and accusing her of teasing the server.

Katherine begged him to lower his voice because he was embarrassing her. Thomas said, "I am embarrassing you – you, whore?" Anger was boiling over.

"Well, I have done a noble duty. Maybe we won't have this issue again."

"What issue?"

"You are spreading your legs with that sexy tone; do you want the server too?" Thomas insinuated.

"No!" Katherine said sarcastically.

"Katherine, I am trying to be as patient as I could with you, and you – never mind, I am about to say something that we both will regret."

"What are you implying Thomas? That speaking with an-other man is not committed enough. Maybe I should pretend that you are the only man on the planet; would that be dedica-tion?"

Thomas sighed deeply and ignored her.

"It's normal for a woman to be kind or speak. At least that is what my parents instilled in me. Besides, I didn't know I needed permission to talk. Maybe the next time I should raise my hand. Or wait for you to choose me to answer the question since I am in class."

"Maybe you should raise your hand, or maybe there won't be the next time, or maybe you should keep your mouth shut, like now. I deserve a woman who respects my decisions. You don't seem like that woman."

"No, I'm not that figurine, and I don't like where this conver-sation is going. Thomas, I think I do need to shut up and leave."

"Leave? Leave? Ha! You'll never leave me, not alive!"

They argued during the whole dinner, and their tensions were high. Thomas was unreasonable.

However, Katherine tried to calm him down. She kissed him on his cheek while they were walking to the car; Thomas turned his head and said to her, "Don't touch me."

When they got in the car, Thomas was yelling in her face. He slapped Katherine on the cheek with an opened hand. It sounded like a loud clap, and then she hit him back.

Katherine started swearing; her face had a red welt. She began honking the horn.

They begin fighting inside the car. Thomas bent Katherine's fingers back to stop her from blowing the horn; Katherine was in so much pain that she became submissive. People were passing by the car, but they were too afraid to knock on the dark tinted glass.

Then he punched her repeatedly; his hand became heavier and stiffer. She held her face as he beat her, and a small cut appeared below her eye. The pain was overbearing. She begged him to stop!

"Stop please stop! Katherine cried out.

However, Thomas kept beating her until she became too afraid to hit back, and Thomas thought he had tamed her. Thomas dropped Katherine off at home without any empathy.

When Katherine got inside, she walked to the mirror to see herself. "I'm so repulsive and ugly," she thought. "Look at me;" she couldn't stand watching her reflection; she didn't recognize the person staring back.

She could not go to school like that. The next day she went into the bathroom and grabbed the foundation to cover her pain and her bruises.

Later, Thomas called Katherine to apologize for losing control. Katherine lured; she begins to think that the fight was a mistake. Thomas was a little bossy and jealous, and his actions were extremely violent.

However, he apologized, and it sounded sincere. He must have been mournful," Katherine thought. Besides, it was better than being lonely.

Katherine was optimistic; she thought Thomas behavior would eventually improve; besides, it was only one fight. Things happen, and people argue; she was naive to the real world.

Later that day, Thomas called Katherine, again he seemed apologetic, and Katherine accepts his apology. Then he made reservations for them to eat at the same restaurant – where they fought.

Katherine was humiliated, but she did not have the strength to fight again. The same waiter came to their table.

However, Katherine allowed Thomas to order her meal and make any decisions. The server glanced at Katherine with sympathy in his eyes. Her face was caked with make-up.

The server did not want to cause another fight. He asked Jason in a bitter tone, "What would you like." Katherine kept her head held down the entire time.

CHAPTER 7

K atherine –

I begin to accept that my life with Thomas was not going to get any better. Pain became a daily routine!

Dear World, I am still winning, I wrote in my journal. I presumed!

I was in a rocky relationship, but it beats being lonely. I was excelling in school.

I earned my bachelor's degree in engineering and a master's degree in Business Administration; my life was classic. It was worth an award.

Then I started staying at work later hours than usual trying to learn all I could about the business, so I could become better than a standard clerk. I worked hard and ultimately worked my way up to become the Chief Executive Officer (CEO) by the age of twenty-three.

My family was proud of me, especially my mother, and I was pleased with myself. Then Thomas begins complaining about the late hours that I worked.

He accused me of eyeing Jason and enticing him with my tight clothing. Thomas was a sick man.

One morning, I had gotten ready for work. I had put on a white bow tie button up blouse with a black blazer. I was in the bedroom mirror looking at myself; I turned around when I heard Thomas come through the door. Thomas saw my shirt, and he ripped it open.

He said, "I can see your bra through that blouse, so choose another color. I'm punishing you because I love you." That was the type of love that every woman desired, right?

I stood there, embarrassed. I pulled my blouse close, but I still felt ashamed. Thomas started calling me ugly, lazy, and fat.

When I examined the mirror that was the image, I heard echoing in my head. He pounded those unkind words into my heart!

I wished I knew how to prevent myself from being so miserable. I hated caring for Thomas.

After Thomas left the bedroom, I started to cry. My arrogance was weakening, and the warning signs of violence were becoming more visible.

However, I was holding onto hope. Nevertheless, I thought Thomas would change. The truth is that I never wore anything appealing to work; it was another one of Thomas' demons.

The idea of another man touching me made Thomas paranoid, and he took it out on me. If Thomas knew that Jason was the man whom I kissed, he would beat me nearly to death and then force me to quit the job. I began wondering if my life was worth living.

Then I began building my life on impulses; I use to share everything with my family and friends. However, things changed – my entire life changed. I couldn't smile anymore, and I crammed hate into my heart until there was no room for anything else to fit.

I was tiptoeing on eggshells. Thomas was unpredictable, a walking human time bomb, which was a half-second from exploding.

Thomas had beaten me until all my love for Jason was almost gone. However, when I saw Jason, I started regaining love and faith again.

"Sadly — I had many buried secrets; Jason, lies, abuse, hate, and no one ever knew about them – not one person.

However, my skeletons could not confine or define me. When I went to work, I pretended to live in another world filled with happiness.

In that imaginary world, the pain didn't exist; it was a world that Thomas could not offend.

Thomas had begun controlling everything: what I wore, what I ate, what time I arrived and left home, and who socialized with me. I began distancing myself from my family and friends, from reality into make-believe.

Thomas started beating me every single day, and it did not matter because I deserved it – that is what he told me, and I eventually started believing. Sometimes he didn't need a reason to hit me; it was just his right, he said.

I was longing to have that freedom again, that feeling that I felt when I first moved out of my parents' home and the way I felt when Thomas was not around – free.

All my dreams were fading away slowly, and so was my freedom. I wanted a soulmate, not a correctional officer. I felt like a criminal in my home; bars surrounded me mentally.

I thought that Thomas was going to suffice; however, things had become so gloomy that I could not distinguish what was realistic anymore. The only things that were loyal in my life were my tears and the pain.

I had built a defensive wall that was well-made. No man could come through it, but my memories for Jason were knocking it down brick by brick.

The pain had replaced my happiness, and my feeling for Thomas was fading away. So, did the reflection in his eyes; it stopped sparkling.

I quickly realize that I had made a tremendous mistake, and Thomas was not the glimmer of love that was in my fantasies. People said, "True Love Will Never Die." Well, something died, or maybe Thomas' love was never right.

I was discovering that Thomas wasn't the dream-love that I desired or deserved, and love was only a fairy-tale. Nevertheless, I held on to my thoughts – my hope that maybe Thomas would change. However, instead, I discovered who I truly loved.

I wondered if they were those secrets that my father spoke of,

I understand now, the reason why my mother did not say anything else about life; it was because it was not her job. It was my father's job to prepare me for those things, such as love, relationships, and men.

I did not listen to all those things, and now I am suffering; I was more interested in acknowledgment and honor. I received the glory that my mother spoke of, but I lost my freedom, dignity, and self-respect.

Just the same, I did not allow my abusive life to stop me from living successfully. I kept pretending as if everything was excellent.

I found me a make-believe Knight; it was Jason, he was in my dreams defending me. He was super tall, with giant muscular arms made of bricks.

I lie down and fall asleep; it was the best part of my life – going to sleep because Thomas could not control me nor my dreams. If Thomas only knew what was going through my mind. He would probably knock it out of me.

When I slept, I was happy and free? Awake or sleep I could not stop loving Jason. However, if I could not retain my love, I may lose my life.

I knew Jason would be the perfect husband, and the more I saw him, the higher my love became.

I was falling in love with him more and more. However, there was a wedge standing between us; it was fear and obligation.

Thomas aggressive behavior frightened me, yet I felt committed. I believed I owed him my heart, life, and soul. However, what terrified me even more; Jason already took them.

Jason supported all my business decisions. Life was different between the two men. While Thomas unpowered me, Jason empowered me. I finally found the glimmer of love that I was searching for, and Jason's passion was effortless. Thomas offered me nothing but a shameful experience. My friends were right.

However, when I began working for Jason, he inspired me to believe in genuine love again, and like always, it was more powerful than I imagined.

I felt as if I belonged to Jason, and I didn't just adore him. I was in love with him even more than before. Besides, he never noticed my scars. I knew if Thomas figured out the truth that I loved Jason, there would be severe consequences.

Thomas was crazy, and I was too afraid to make him angry. I could not take another swollen, black, and blue eye, bloody nose, or purple bruise. Thomas knuckles stained by my blood, but it never stopped him from hitting me. Pain destroyed my heart!

CHAPTER 8

atherine –

I saw Jason at my recitals and then the prom. Afterward, Jason and I had gone to dinner, and later, we had a picnic in the park.

Everything was fantastic until Marcy Sterling intruded. She was interested in Jason.

She was a size one, twine thin, shapely figured much smaller than I. She had a cheerful attitude; it was a little too cheery for my liking.

Her voice was sugary – sweet and charming. She had an evil – crooked smile. She wore mid-thigh skirts that revealed her long brown ebony legs.

Her shirts were above her belly button; you can almost iron clothing on her waistline. There was no fat anywhere on Marcy's body.

Marcy was known for grasping the attention of men. She was good at it.

The first time, I laid eyes on my mysterious admirer, Jason; it was at my recital. I enjoyed my poesy performances; they were every Thursday night.

The most considerable part of it was when Jason arrived at 8:00 pm, faithfully. He sat on the front row seats during each recital.

I always gawked at him, as I read my poems; he seized my entire mind, and I believe I held his'. When I finished, he stood up and gave me a standing ovation as he scrutinized my performance; awe-struck by my words.

Marcy was sitting next to him. I hated her with envy! She was continually whispering in Jason's ear as they laughed together through the performance.

Marcy's hand gripping his' muscular thigh as she rudely distracted him. Slyly rubbing between his legs, "Ahem" I coughed on the stage, it seemed like I needed a glass of water to keep me from choking. If I didn't have such an ethical background, it would have been her neck that I was bracing.

While Marcy stared at me with that victorious stare, which intimidated me, I stared at Jason with a cautious stare, one that said leave that witch alone if you wish to be with me.

I had no clue why I had so many emotions for this guy. Was I in love with him?

I was always curious, who was he? The well dressed, tall, athletic-looking, mysterious student who listened to me as I recited poems?

One of my best friends', Katie Randall dated his best friend, Walter Sanchez. Since Jason and Walter were best friends, I asked Katie weeks ago who this mysterious guy was.

"I don't know much about the shadowy guy, but his first name is Jason. Katie said."

Jason, I think – I have a crush on Jason. We laughed. So, who is his girlfriend?

"He does not have one."

Interesting! Well, who's that witch that's always with him?

"The witch name is Marcy, and the rumors are – she's eager to sleep in his bed."

Jason –

I have gone to every one of Katherine's poetry performances. At least that's the name; they announced just before she walked out to perform.

I idolized her, although, I was willing to sleep with Marcy. I questioned if Katherine was interested in me; it did not seem like it. She never approached me.

Therefore, I pondered! Should I gamble, stake it all with Katherine or value the opportunity that Marcy was offering. However, there was another dilemma; I was in love with Katherine.

Although Marcy was sexy as hell, she wasn't Katherine. But her pillow talk was very alluring.

Marcy's sweet lips tasted like peaches; she was a great kisser. Her aroma was a pleasant scent of May flowers. Her skin was tender; her long silky legs were glossy.

She was tempting my manhood. I freshly remember when she walked up to me and sat on my lap. Face to face, we stared at each other. Then she begins bouncing up and down, teasing me.

It was difficult holding on to love when it was versus lust. I sought Marcy; however, I couldn't hurt Katherine.

Well –

Katherine wrote extraordinary poems. They were persuasive. The portrayal of the coldness! The heartbreaks, the love, and the warmness that she expressed through her words were terrific:

My favorite poem was;

My True Love

The tears
The loneliness
The fears – the doubts
The Insecurities, the lack of trust
The pain, the heartbreaks
The hopelessness
The Whispers, pleas
They were all heard

And you came without hesitation
Without attachments
Without limitations
Without a purpose
You came with honor, friendship, and strength
You came with unquestionable and unconditional love
At that precise moment and you filled that void
With endless love

Katherine –

March 29, 2005

My mother and I went to Elite's Finest Formal Clothing Mall. I went from store to store searching for hours for an elegant prom dress.
I was about to give up until I looked up at the display window at Marie's Boutique. I smiled!
A lovely outfit had grasped my attention. It was stunning.

Wow –

This is the one!" A gorgeous, smooth, red velvet mermaid skirt was on display.
The tail of the skirt dragged the floor, and the front was scarcely below the knee. The blouse was red; lace and lavishing satin.
I wanted to take Jason's eyes off Marcy and focus them on me. This outfit seemed like the perfect defense.
I walked into the store while mum walked throughout the mall. I continued to speak to the store clerk, Gabby.
I tried on the skirt and then the blouse; it was a perfect fit. I looked incredible. mum returned just in time, she walked over to the counter and paid for the dress, and then we left.

◆ ◆ ◆

Saturday, April 24, 2005

It was Sumter Time High School senior prom. It was finally here; Katherine was ecstatic; it was a notable night!

The most significant moment of the year and nothing — nothing was going to ruin Katherine's lovely night not even Marcy.

Katherine went to the salon; she waited patiently for the stylist. Ten minutes after she arrived, the hairstylist shouted her name.

Michelle introduced herself. Katherine rushed to the chair, and then she flopped down. She was thrilled and worried at the same time!

She could not picture the beauty of herself. She desired to be much prettier than Marcy, and she begins thinking awful thoughts:

"What if something goes wrong, or Michelle cuts my hair too short? Or dyes it a ridiculous color, or doesn't do a great job? What if I am not beautiful enough?"

Michelle styled Katherine's hair. Katherine was impatient and anxiously waiting to see herself in the mirror.

Michelle began asking Katherine questions; she was trying to help Katherine relax; however, nothing was working as far as Katherine was concerned, especially when she saw Marcy preparing to be just as pretty.

"So, what's the special occasion?" Michelle asked.

Katherine glimmered. "It's prom night!"

"Do you have a date?"

"No!"

"So, you are telling me that not one guy makes you smile!"

"Jason, he is adorable and handsome with cute dimples."

"But does he make you smile," Michele said with a humungous grin on her face.

Katherine chuckles! "Every Thursday evening, I smile. I – I tingle when I see him. It feels as if butterflies are flapping their wings inside my stomach. I see him, and I become woozy with excitement, and when I don't, I feel as if a storm cloud is above my head, and I miss him greatly!

Then if anything or anyone attempt to jeopardize our relations I become – defensive. So, does it sound like I get excited?"

"It sounds like you are in love! Is he handsome?"

"Is he? He is drop-dead, lip-smacking gorgeous!"

"Well Katherine let's impress this tasty man and when I finish; your reflection would be exquisiteness at its sunniest. You will look magnificent, and I bet all the boys would love to be with you!" Michelle kept combing Katherine's hair.

"I appreciate the compliment Michelle, but I doubt if I'll excite all the boys. Besides I don't want them all, I only need to amaze Jason. Then make his jaw drop and entreat me to give him kisses."

Michelle handed Katherine the mirror. Katherine snickered! Her eyes enlarged as her reflection glistened at her.

Katherine stutters "I-I am pretty!" Pretty is an understatement Michelle said, "No, you – you are gorgeous!" Katherine smiles!

Katherine looks in the mirror, unblemished and arresting is what Katherine saw reflecting towards her. She was a modest beauty. However, so was Marcy?

Katherine's hair was long, smooth, and radiant. The wavy hair sat on her shoulders, and when Katherine turned her head, the black, silky hair bounced and swayed.

Kathrine's smile sparkled brighter than the midnight stars. Her smile was sunlight!

Katherine's full lips were red and glossy. Her eyeshadow was silver and glittery; she looked resplendent.

Katherine's eyebrows were arched and traced with black eyeliner. She grinned from ear to ear; her beauty revived; her eyes brightened as she flaunted in the mirror! She was the three S's: sumptuous, sexy, and stunning; she could not stop gazing at herself in the mirror.

Marcy sat three seats away from Katherine. Her teeth shined as she smiled. She wore red berry lipstick on her smooth pouting lips.

Her hair was golden, curly, and bouncy. She had arched eyebrows and velvety black lashes.

Marcy was also ready to astound Jason, and she looked as if she was prepared to win.

Katherine left the salon. Mrs. Roosevelt's seat leaned back; she was reading a book. She noticed Katherine prancing towards the car; she saw the true spirit of a homecoming queen.

Masterpiece—

Mrs. Roosevelt inhaled a deep breath, and then she sat up. Katherine opened the door, and Mrs. Roosevelt said – "You are a sparkling, shining, gold medal, with a cutting edge!"

Conceitedly, Katherine responds, "So, you noticed that too, mum." Then she smacked her lips and tossed her hair.

Mrs. Roosevelt looked at her and said, "What have your father and I created." Katherine giggled and then said, "A passionate young lady with confidence."

Mrs. Roosevelt smiled; she was proud of Katherine.

Katherine was excited and, in a rush, to get home and dressed before 7:00 pm.

Katherine –

I arrived at home; I started getting dressed. I laid the outfit on the bed; I bathed.

Forty minutes later, I got out of the tub and patted myself dry. Next, I showered my body with softly scented flora perfume.

Then I slid into the red well-designed satin lace blouse; my soft young shoulders were showing through the clothing. I wiggle into the elegant red velvet skirt.

It was skintight; however, it complimented my curvy body and enticing hips. I rubbed softly scented lotion on my face, neck, and then my legs.

I slipped into a pair of stylish white heels with red hearts, pearls, and roses – a perfect combination of love. I was standing in the mirror, turning from side to side, admiring my hourglass body.

I was fine-looking and nicely built with thick thighs, a small waistline, and a handful of breasts. I was sashaying in the bedroom mirror; my mother called me. I trotted downstairs; she hugged and kissed me, and then squeezed me tightly!

She handed me a gift box. I ripped the paper from the package and opened the container.

"Wow" – it was a white pearl necklace, with two medium-sized red hearts. There was a white rose planted between each heart. The piece of jewelry was very detailed.

The word "Love" connected both hearts to the rose. Love brought life to my soul, and the rose as well.

My mother fastened the unique necklace around my neck; it went well with my attire and perfect with my heels.

The chain was lovely. Everything seemed to match extremely well. I felt gorgeous!

"I love you," Mother said!

Jason –

Enchanting — it was the day of the prom. Marcy asked me if I would go with her. She was a gorgeous girl, and any man would have said, "Yes."

However, my eye was on a bigger prize, Katherine Roosevelt.

Walter and I went to the barbershop to get a haircut and then we went to my house to get dressed.

All the things that I had done or prepared for were for "Katherine." I wanted to impress this Katherine Roosevelt.

Katie had given me Katherine's prom colors, and of course, I chose the same ones. My tuxedo and the corsage were red and white; it coordinated precisely with Katherine's attire.

I stood in the mirror, getting dressed. As I straightened my tie; I wondered how I could make this night the most whimsical night of Katherine's life.

I wanted to give Katherine the most delicate things in life, and as I stood in the mirror admiring my looks, I realized, "I am the finest."

I stood tall, 5'10 and a half, with broad shoulders and muscular arms. When I gazed into the mirror, I beamed, because I was so handsome. Yes, I was tooting my own horn and anxiously waiting to see Katherine.

Katherine –

Mum said, "Go and have fun, the limo is waiting;" I glimpsed out of the living room window; a large white SUV was sitting in the driveway.

"The greatest night of my life," I yelled loudly. Then dashed outside and opened the passenger side door.

I peeped inside the limo. My eyes lit up; it was flawless. I lifted the tail of my skirt; I stepped into the limo, and then I took a seat. I felt like Cinderella searching for a prince, however with my luck, I would probably catch a frog, I thought.

My cell phone begins ringing; it's Katie.

"Hello! Katherine, where are you?"

I am almost there.

"Can you sit on the passenger side; the side that's closer to the school?"

Yes!

The chauffeur arrived at Summertime High School to pick up my friends; Katie, Walter, Maryann, and Michael.

When I arrived at the school, the group was standing next to the surprise guest, Jason Taylor. I did not have a date apparently neither did he.

My smile lit up like a bright light bulb. I felt as if I had won his heart.

I was glowing when I saw his face! I was pleased to see the young man.

Jason climbed into the limo and sat next to me. He moved closer and closer towards me.

My heart felt as if it was pounding against my chest [dup – dup, dup — dup]; I stopped breathing for a second.

I needed a fan; things were becoming intense. I was edgy, and I could not sit still.

Jason was well-groomed, cleanly shaven with trimmed nails. He smelled incredible, but he made me feel jittery.

We had on the same matching colors. Everything seemed odd; it was a strange coincidence, or was it by fluke? I wondered.

Jason handed me a corsage with red and white roses. I knew then that Katie or Maryann had planned everything because certain things were too accidental.

I wondered how Jason knew; my favorite flower was a rose, and my favorite color was red.

Although I held back the tears with my mother. I could not hold them back when Jason handed me the corsage.

"My love, why are you crying?"

I – I don't know!

Jason got a Kleenex and patted away my tears; he did not want the tears to ruin my make-up, neither did I.

I desired to say, "I love you!" I wanted to keep crying because he had touched my heart, but I could not.

Then Jason opened the container and removed the corsage from the box and placed it on my left wrist.

"Forever in Love" by Kenny G. was playing on the radio. I could not explain my emotions or what was happening to my heart.

"Was the music touching it or love?" I wondered! I had never experienced such feelings before.

Katie walked up to the limo and introduced us, "Jason, this is my best friend, Katherine Roosevelt."

"Hello Katherine, it's a pleasure to meet you finally!"

Hi, Jason it's nice to meet you as well.

Jason reached for my hand and placed the palm of it against his hand. Then he kissed it softly!

I closed my eyes; because my heart skipped another beat. Jason stared at me, and then he kissed my hand again; my posture was rigid.

I could not look into his eyes; instead, my head drooped. A

man had never touched me before in that manner. However, his touch made my body shiver all over.

Jason –

Katherine was not expecting me! When the limo stopped, Katie and I walked towards it. Then I opened Katherine's door.

Katherine could not take her eyes off me, enticed by them, I could not turn away. Katherine was glaring!

I sat beside her and then reached for her wrist. I put the corsage around it.

Soft music was playing; I felt an electrifying feeling that pulled me toward her like a magnet. Strange emotions were rushing through my body; I had never experienced anything like this before.

Katherine's kiss was more potent than Marcy's lap dances; I was afraid of what she could do with one bounce.

Although I was eighteen, I had never been with a woman sexually. Katherine was my first real date.

We arrived at the banquet hall. I hopped out of the limo and grabbed Katherine by the arm to help her down. I was still staring in her eyes.

Before we went inside, we took group and individual pictures. We also took pictures with our dates. We were standing up straight posing for the camera.

Since Katherine and I did not have a partner, we took pictures together. I was surprised how Katherine had become fond of me already!

After two pictures, Marcy walked up to me and insisted on standing between the two of us. Katherine was furious; she walked away.

Katherine –

I walked through the wooden doors strutting and dancing to the music. I was angry, but I remained hopeful!

Jason made me feel like the most important woman in the

world and the only one who ever mattered until Marcy arrived.

I pranced inside of the ballroom and began dancing with Maryann and Katie. However, where was Jason? I mumbled under my breath.

I had lost sight of him in the crowd. I turned my head and looked around; however, I did not see him. I veered toward Maryann, and then I yelled.

"Have you seen Jason?"

"No!"

Neither did Katie.

Then I looked up and saw him and Marcy grinding each other as they danced. I wanted to cry; my heart saddened by love and broken into a trillion pieces. I turned my back.

After the song was over, I felt a soft tap against my shoulder. I turned around; my face skewed for a second as I stared at him.

Jason came and stood close in front of me. My eyes were watery. Jason didn't understand why there were tears in my eyes. I don't think he even knew I cared.

I bit down on the bottom of my lip, and then I turned my head and smiled. However, I was still facing Jason; he was tall, and he mounted over me.

Jason asked me, "May I have this dance?"

I blushed and said, "Yes!"

The DJ played; "My Girl" by The Temptations, I rested my hand and head against Jason's wooden chest. Although he could not hold a note, he was whispering the words of the song into my ear.

I tilted my head towards Jason's mouth. We rocked from side to side. Jason glided across the floor with me inside his arms; he kept chanting "My Girl."

Jason tipped my head back as he gave me a subtle kiss on my soft full lips. It was a remarkable moment; my soul was beginning to connect with his'.

My feelings were becoming more and more powerful, and my emotions were dominating my body. Our erotic urges were taking over.

We were playing with fire, and we were walking straight into the flames. Jason and I were in love, but neither one of us was ready for it.

Jason was a polite, handsome, respectful young man who pampered me as if I was his actual date. I was falling in love with a boy that I barely knew.

Then Marcy stepped in, "Can I borrow him," she asked. I wanted to say, "You could borrow this fist, you witch; however, my mother did not raise me to be disrespectful."

Jason –

We finally arrived at the banquet hall. Katherine was dancing as she walked through the doors. I loved her poised attitude; it was very desirable!

Once she got inside, she began dancing with her friends. I was watching her as she looked around; she was searching for someone, perhaps me.

However, I was dancing with Marcy; she was bending down, her lower body was brushing against my penis. I grabbed her around her waistline and pulled her closer.

Suddenly, I became aroused and I had to leave quickly before I made the biggest mistake of my life. I walked up to Katherine; tears were in her eyes.

What's wrong? I asked.

"Nothing!"

I asked her to join me on the dance floor. I rendered my hand to her, and then Katherine placed the palm of her hand inside mine.

I pulled her closer to me. Then I led her to the middle of the dance floor.

I put my fingers between her fingers. I pulled Katherine closer to me. I noticed her arms covered with goosebumps.

"Are you cold?"

"No, quite the opposite, I am steaming inside."

Katie and Walter were dancing next to us. However, they

were distracted. Katherine and I had caught everyone's attention. You could feel our love sparkling in the air.

Everyone stopped dancing; suddenly they began watching us as we moved across the floor. I did not have a clue about sex, but I desired Katherine sexually, even more than Marcy.

However, rumors had spread around the school that Katherine wasn't having sex until she was married. But I felt as if I was ready for sex.

Katherine was my only interest, and I wanted to steal just one kiss from her while we were dancing. I did not care if other girls were watching me on the dance floor.

I loved Katherine, and she clutched all my thoughts. I could not concentrate; everything about Katherine Roosevelt felt sincere. I held Katherine in my arms tightly as we pranced around the dance floor.

I did not want the music to stop or let Katherine go – ever. I craved to kiss her lips desperately; I pulled her closer to me. I leaned my head down; her face was against my face.

I know she felt my erected penis against her body. However, she never gave any signs that she was interested in going any further.

Then I lifted Katherine into the air as high as I could and spun her around; she soared in the air. The lights from the cameras flashed as the photographer took our pictures.

It was a breathtaking moment, and I savored the seconds. I desired Katherine, and I wanted her to become my wife one day.

Katherine –

I was anticipating on becoming the Homecoming Queen, and I wondered who would be chosen to be my king; I wished that it was Jason.

I worked extremely hard at school, trying to gain that title. I was hoping my hard work paid off.

The prom was magical. It started in the limo when I first laid my eyes on Jason. My heart crippled by his love. OH, the erotic feelings that I felt! Especially when he kissed me; it was incredible.

My eyes remained focused on Jason! I was beginning to wonder what should come first in my life – school or him. I did not choose my education as usual.

The music stopped; it was finally time to announce the king and the queen. The presenter reads the card and called out loudly JASON TAYLOR; they elected him as the homecoming king. Everyone applauded!

My hand was trembling; I was yearning to know who they had chosen to be his Queen. It was sixty seconds of silence, tick – tock, tick – tock, tick – tock, and time was gradually passing.

I was sitting in the chair leaning forward fidgeting with my fingers and then I crossed them. Each second seemed like a minute.

I clutched Maryann and Katie's wrist and squeezed it tightly. I was praying, "Pl-please, pick me!"

One minute appeared as if thirty minutes had gone by, and then the host shouted, "KATHERINE ROOSEVELT."

I forgot that I was a woman or a queen. I hollered, screamed, jumped up and down.

I finally calmed down. I took a deep breath. I sprinted up to the stage to receive my crown and roses.

The announcer crowned me, the Queen of Homecoming; however, the most precious moment is when they announced me as Jason's Queen.

I smiled and waved at the crowd. Then I winked my eye at Marcy. Katie and Maryann were happy for me. They cheered again!

Afterward, the DJ played Jason's favorite song, "May I have this Dance" by Francis and the Lights; it was time for the homecoming queen and king to dance. Jason started dancing like a professional dancer, and he made all the right moves.

He grabbed me by the hand. We were on the stage; I shook my head, "No, no, and no," I said.

The beat is way too fast for me. My dancing skills were amateurish and clumsy.

I was slightly shy, and I did not want to embarrass myself or him on the dance floor. However, Jason forbids me from walking off the stage. We were mumbling and arguing.

He held me in his arms firmly and pulled me closer towards him. Then he gripped my hand snugly. I stared into his eyes.

"You're not leaving, Jason whispered."

Yes, I am!

Jason squeezed my hand tighter. Then he murmured in my ear and repeated it, "You're not leaving!"

Jason, the beat is way too fast.

Jason kissed me on the cheek and then said, "I will guide you. Just trust me."

I trust you!

Jason wrapped me in his arms like an angel with wings, and we began dancing. I draped my arms around Jason's neck and embraced him; I felt safe there.

I began slowly tapping my feet to the beat of the music. Jason was smiling and staring at me!

It felt a little awkward to be in love with a boy; I never imagined myself ever dating a man, not until I was at least thirty. Furthermore, dancing in front of a crowd made me feel more and more nervous; however, Jason's touch was gratifying, delightful, and comforting.

My bashfulness was slowly fading away. I walked around Jason in a full circle, moving my hips as I shimmed; my hair was bouncing. Then I came to a complete stop. My back was against his firm chest; I started jiggling my ass to the beat, my waist was jerking and twirling.

"Katherine, what happened to that shy girl?"

You have roused the monster that's within her.

Jason smiled and spun me around in circles, and he begins swiftly moving across the floor, with me in his arms. We were staring intensely at one another, and our desires were dictating our movements. My heartbeat felt as if it was beating with the rhythm of the music.

Jason suddenly lifts me in the air; my mind was spinning in circles; I was dizzy from love; my heart was drifting away. The crowd was excited!

I loved him! I had found the love of my life, and he was gorgeous and sexy.

Jason –

I stumbled into the prettiest girl in town. Now, it was time for the last dance, right before the speaker announced the homecoming king and queen.

Katherine had romanced me, and I had fallen head over hills in love with her. Katherine was the first lady that I ever desired or loved.

She was the dream date, with her picture-perfect smile, the lovely smell of her perfume, the softness of her smooth hair, and her caring attitude.

My darling Katherine had charmed me. Instead of me sweeping her off her feet, she had swept me off mines.

After we danced, it was time for them to announce the homecoming king and queen. Everyone was looking at the announcer.

They called my name first; I walked up front, pounding my hands against my chest as if I was the king of the jungle. There were dozens of beautiful women in the crowd, including Marcy, but only one that I desired to be my queen—there was only one girl that captivated me.

I was patiently waiting for them to call her name. I had already chosen Katherine to be my queen, but I needed everyone else to agree with my decision.

Then they said 'Katherine Roosevelt'; my eyes blinked. It took a half of a second for everything to sink in. My heart was overwhelmed. Katherine ran to the center of the stage. When she got there, a tear fell from my eyes, and she wiped it away with her thumb. She was happy, so was I!

The crowd and I laughed and clapped because of her juvenile

behavior. It was time for the last dance; the beat was slightly fast.

I decided to dance with her right there on the stage. I wanted everyone to see the girl that I relished. Katherine was breathing heavily!

"Are you tired," I asked her?

"No, I'm just excited!"

I extended my hand, but Katherine was too afraid to clutch it.

I walked up to her and invited her to dance with me. I promised Katherine that I would not let go of her.

Nevertheless, she needed to trust me. Once she did, I wrapped my hands around Katherine's waist and pulled her closer towards me. Her breast leaned tightly against my chest.

I wanted to touch the lower parts of her body impishly; however, I had to control my desires. Katherine was an extraordinary lady!

The more we danced, the more airless it became, and the deeper her breaths became. In the middle of the dance, I completely stopped; I gazed into Katherine's eyes for about ten seconds, I needed to cherish the moment.

Then I picked Katherine up again and twirled her around. She was so beautiful and perfect; no other words could fit her.

After the dance and prom was over, we all got back into the limo. Katherine's stomach growled, "I'm starving, I wish the chauffeur would drive a little faster," she said.

We arrived at Moseley's Luxury Restaurant, one of the most elegant restaurants in town. Katherine had made reservations there three weeks before the prom.

The waiter walked us to the nearest table. I pulled out Katherine's chair. She sat down; I spread the napkin across her lap.

Then I pushed Katherine's chair back to the table. I sat next to her.

Katherine is everything okay? I asked her.

"Everything is magnificent!"

Katherine ordered roasted garlic steak and a potato. I offered to cut up her meat, and she handed me the plate. I slightly brushed my hand against her hand when I moved the plate.

Katherine looked up, and then we gazed into each other's eyes, we were in love. I picked up the knife and the fork; then I sliced Katherine's meat; I fed her a small piece of the steak and potato.

She was eating; but she paused. I shouted out her name. "KATHERINE!" However, she never even heard my voice until I tapped her on the arm.

"I am sorry!"

Are you okay? You were in a daze.

"Yes, I am okay!"

So, what were you thinking about?

"Wouldn't you like to know?"

So, you were thinking about me?

"No!"

Katherine, you lie very well. I know you have feelings for me.

"I do not have feelings for you."

Katherine, you are lying again.

"Jason, let us eat."

Then I pushed the plate back towards her. We were sitting at the table eating. It was silent.

I looked at her as she ate; I enjoyed seeing her facial expressions, especially when she was satisfied, and it showed. Katherine dropped her head, but I hated seeing her so timid.

I reached over and lifted Katherine's head with one finger. Then I told her, the only one who could look down on you is God, and he's the only one that you should look up to.

After we finished eating; I went to the counter to pay for our meals.

"I have my own money." Katherine said.

Keep it, I told her.

Before we walked outside, I grabbed some mints, just in case she kissed me goodnight. We got back into the limo. Katherine laid her head against my shoulder. I rubbed her hand.

Whatever Katherine needed or desired, I made sure it was hers'. I did not need to offer her the world, what would that do for her if she only wished for me?

I wanted to make Katherine happy, and give her exactly what she wanted; maybe she wasn't ready to handle the world, not just yet.

That evening was a night to remember. It was everything!

Katherine –

I felt a cold shiver against my legs as Jason spreads the napkin across them. The stiff breeze felt as if it came from the cold touch of Jason's hand.

Jason had excellent etiquette manners. I ordered my meal and Jason offered to cut it up.

I was eating; but I paused and then started daydreaming. I dreamed that I was walking down the aisle with Jason, hand, and hand, and tears were pouring from my eyes.

I was more focused on Jason than dinner. My love was intensifying to a level that took complete control of my thoughts.

I took a few more small bites; the food was excellent. I noticed Jason staring at me, as usual.

After we finished eating, we went to the counter. Jason removed his expensive leather wallet from his pocket.

I had never met anyone like Jason before. I felt superior! I did not want the night to end.

I didn't want to leave. Our love felt more unyielding when we were together.

Before Jason got out of the limo, he leaned over and whispered into my ear, "What is your phone number?"

I felt the heat from his warm minty breath against my face; I desired to kiss his lips; my mouth was watering. But I was afraid.

Jason –

I inhaled a mouthful of air, swallowed, and then I licked my dry lips. I felt the chemistry glistening.

I turned my face towards Katherine. Then parted my lips and so did Katherine. Our lips locked; we begin kissing intensely.

I kissed Katherine passionately; it lasted for about thirty long seconds. I felt a tingling sensation that embraced my body. Damn!

Katherine –

I licked and sucked my lips. Then I coughed. "Ahem!" I attempted to give Jason my phone number. "Um, 860...85—...no 583", but I could barely get the numbers out.

Afterward, I went home; and fell across the sofa; I saw millions and millions of stars hovering above me. I told my sisters and my mother, "I'm in love, and it's deep – it's deep."

They smirked; because they knew I had never desired a boy before until this night. "That boy must have impressed you. You better be careful," mother said.

She did not want me to get off track of my schoolwork. Perhaps mother should have been more disturbed about other things. However, my education and success were her most relevant concern.

Jason –

I could not sleep; the night was restless. Katherine's arms wrapped around my neck, and her soft skin was all that I thought about as I lay in the bed.

The next morning, I decided to make plans for Katherine and me. I called Katherine.

"Good morning, how are you?"

"Good morning Jason, I'm fine!" She replied in a raspy tone.

"Did I wake you?"

"Yes, you did!"

"I apologize! However, I called you to see if you could meet me at Lake Cherry Blossom at noon."

"Yes!"

"Great, I will see you there!"

"Okay!"

I wanted to surprise Katherine with a picnic in the park, just the two of us. I called Walter, and Michael to assist me with setting things up.

While Katherine and I were home getting dressed, they went to the park hours before Katherine and me. Katie and Maryann went with them. After they were done setting up everything they left.

I arrived at the park right before Katherine. I needed to check out the scenery, and it was romantic.

A white blanket spread across the grass, and several pink throw pillows were on top of the cover. Propped against the tree trunk, next to the quilt was a small coffee table.

Different fruits were on a large square platter. Dips and spreads were in bowls. Chocolate dipped strawberries, and desserts were on top of the expensive dinnerware. Red wine poured into champagne glasses.

Katherine appears a couple of hours later; I was waiting for her arrival. I walked up to Katherine, and I kissed her on the cheek. She had on a pair of black jogging shorts, a t-shirt, and sandals.

Her toenails were freshly polished, and she looked sexy. She was the physical version of the perfect African American doll.

We strolled towards a large Cherry Blossom tree. The scent of floral perfumes covered the park ground. Pink and white petals were falling on the ground onto the blanket.

Katherine was quite surprised; with her mouth slightly opened. I was thinking naughty thoughts; I wanted her legs gapped open, but I had to wait and be patient until she became my wife.

It was fascinating! She was nearly in tears. She lay on the blanket, and I sat beside her. I fixed two small plates, and then we ate, and we talked – well, she spoke, and I watched her. She wanted to confess her true feelings, but she was afraid.

Katherine –

Jason, I need a man who can turn my whole world around

in one heartbeat [dup]. Someone who can kiss me passionately, touch me tenderly and hold me tightly, until I believe that true love does exist.

I need you to know everything about me and all my insecurities, fears, doubts, and pain.

If you desire a queen, I am her. However, I need a gracious King, and if I have that – I will never leave you.

I need you, Jason; I need your love and your strength. I need you to put my fears and insecurities to sleep.

I never realized how deeply I loved you until now. I want us to become united as light is to brightness, and I want our love to shine brighter than the sunlight."

I don't want you ever to find a lady who could love you as much as I do. Furthermore, I want you to be the only man who could soothe my flames – my body when it is raging out of control.

Jason –

Katherine, I want us to have a relationship that is as solid as a rock. Cold as an iced lake, hot as hell; I ask for more than any man. I demand to be first.

I stared at Katherine with infatuation in my eyes. I sneaked a kiss now and then, her lips were soft and silky, and the fourth kiss was better than the first, second, and third kisses.

Katherine –

"Let's go to the park and take a walk," Jason said. I remember walking across the arched bridge holding hands and getting to know one another. Jason asked me if I had brought a second set of clothing, and I said, "Yes."

Suddenly, I felt his hand bump against my shoulder. I screamed as he shoved me across the small bridge into the water.

Then he jumped into the lake behind me. I suppose he leaped into the water just in case he had to save me.

I tumbled into the icy cold water, "Ow," I uttered. It splashed. I sunk deep into the water.

I held my breath until I was nearly blue in the face. I wondered how long it would take Jason to save me; then Jason immediately swam under and grabbed me.

He wrapped his sturdy arm around my waist and pulled me up. I pretended to be unconscious, as soon as we were above the water, he turned my body towards him. I suppose he wanted to resuscitate me.

I was waiting for the exact moment to see him face to face, and when I did, I started pounding my hands against the freezing water. His face was dripping wet from the splashes.

Jason let go of me and then he wiped his face with the palm of his hands. I swam to the edge of the water, and then I stood up.

I started running around the lake. Jason chased me until he caught me, precisely what I wanted. He stared at me more profound than ever, and he didn't blink, neither did I.

He grabbed me from the rear and then wrapped his arms above my waist. He spun me around, and both of us fell into the lake.

He fell on top of me. He softly kissed the back of my neck. Then he drew the curves of my back as he dragged his tongue down my spine.

He ran his tongue across the hind of my bikini to the back of my thigh; then he kissed the inside of it. I felt an exciting, chilling sensation in parts of my body that I never knew existed, and chill bumps ran down my spine.

My vagina was throbbing. Jason stopped and sat up. He heaves a slight sigh; the pressure from his penis was inflating through his shorts. My mind was cloudy, curious to find out what was under the puffed-up clothing.

A few hours later, it was time for us to leave; Jason covered me with a large beach towel. However, I was still shivering from his touch.

I walked to the restroom to change my clothing. I put on a v-cut, sunflower sundress, with thin straps.

I returned, I lay down, and Jason handed me a gift bag; I looked inside.

It was a personalized pillow with a picture of Jason and me. He was lifting me high in the air. It was one of the images taken at the prom.

"Thank you! How did you get this picture so quickly?"

Jason grinned. "You're welcome and I have connections."

Jason –

I stared brazenly into Katherine's eyes; they looked cold. However, I knew that I could soften them.

I asked Katherine, who wants to love – like an empty glass? Who desires a broken heart?

A heart that's incapable of being fixed; insufficient feelings and a heart shattered into pieces? Who wants sunshine with no warmth?

I want to flirt with you every day. I want to tell you every day that – I love you! I want to hug you – kiss you every single day.

I do not want you ever to be afraid to love me, never be terrified to come to me. When you are in pain, I never want you to panic about our relationship. My job is to protect you, and I will die doing it.

I desire to give you the affection that no other man could give you. You should never have to worry about my love for you or feel guilty for loving me.

If things get so cold that it freezes my heart, I need you to be able to beat the ice until it breaks the barrier. Stick with me, and I promise you that you will never regret it. My love – my beloved, I love you, and I will tell the world."

Katherine –

I felt alive; we went back home; I guess everything was just prom amity. Now, I needed to concentrate on schoolwork again, but my feelings for Jason were nagging me. I was in love, and it was deep!

My world stopped when he kissed me. I felt feelings that were so powerful that they overtook my soul. I experienced a love that traveled more deep-rooted than the underworld, and it penetrated in complexity more significant than I could tolerate.

It trapped my mind, body, and soul. It was so pleasing and authentic that I could not speak nor move; it was an intoxication that made me stagger to the ground.

Jason astounded me with each kiss. Love was better than any love I had ever dreamed of and sweeter than all the desserts that I have ever tasted.

CHAPTER 9

J ason –

After the picnic, I had gone home. However, my penis still needed some attention. I am embarrassed, and I admit, I called Marcy, and she came over right away.

My parents were gone; I invited her into my bedroom. She said, "I know what you need."

Then give it to me, I said. Marcy kissed me with those peachy lips. They tasted as good as the first day that I felt them.

I wanted to stop her, but my body needed to be touched by a woman. I wanted it to be Katherine; however, she wasn't ready for sex.

Marcy continued to kiss me. I slide Marcy's pants off and then her blouse.

Her titties were just enough to nib on, and they were as sweet as strawberries. I laid her on my bed and rested on top of her.

I inserted my penis inside of her and then began pounding her vagina as fast as I could. I was thinking about Katherine the entire time.

I had lost control of my body. The inside of Marcy' vagina was warm and moist.

I was moaning, and so was she, the touch of her body felt beautiful. I exploded inside of her. We laid there for a second then I asked her to leave.

After I showered, I called Katherine to tell her goodnight. While I was on the phone, Marcy called, I did not answer.

I wanted nothing else to do with her – having sex with her was a regretful mistake.

Marcy kept calling the phone; it kept beeping. Once I hung up with Katherine, I answered and asked her to stop calling me.

She was upset and threatened to tell Katherine the truth. So, I continued to see her and have sex with her.

Katherine –

I desired to become a bigtime executive, and nothing was going to destroy my aspirations, not even Jason. Summertime High School was one of the best schools in the country and well known for guiding students toward their dreams.

I had huge ones and being with Jason was one of my illusions. Although, I woke up each morning with a big-hearted smile, and Jason's picture stuck against my sweaty face.

I knew walking away from Jason was crucial. Especially when rumors were going around that he and Marcy were having sex, although he denied it.

Love was obliviously taking over, and the rumors were ruining my life – breaking my heart. I was beginning to neglect my responsibilities, such as school.

It is evident that I had fallen in love faster than I expected, and I was becoming irresponsible. After five months of dating Jason, I chose to make a hasty decision.

However, I did not know if I was strong enough to go through with it. I called Jason and asked him if he could meet me at our favorite café [Lovers Lane, Coffee, and Kisses]. Two hours later, we arrived at the same time.

I parked, sat in the car, crying. Jason walked up to the car and then opened the driver's side door where I was sitting. Tears were pouring down my cheek.

"What's wrong darling?"

Your smile, smell, touch, eyes — everything about you is perfect. However, Marcy called me; she's pregnant.

You said you were waiting; furthermore, you said that you

loved me. I can't do this anymore.

"Can't what?"

Live like this, continue to love like this!

"Like what Katherine, I don't understand! What's wrong?"

It's over!

[Ba – Bum, Jason's heart pounds!] "What's over?" More tears fell down his cheek! "Don't do this to me, Katherine!"

Did you hear me? Marcy is pregnant; it's over!

[Ba – Bum his heart pounds again.] "No! I will not accept it. I don't care if she is pregnant. It is not that simple; it's quite impossible to let go of you."

For me, yes! It – is just that easy. Just let go!

"Do you… – Have you ever known what love meant? Do you think I – I can stop loving you overnight? Again, it is impossible!"

Jason –

Ba – Bum, my soul, was slowly dying. I attempted to place one hand on the door; it slipped, I felt dizzy.

I leaned down towards Katherine's face; I gaze at her. Ba - Bum, my heart begins pound frantically again and again.

Pl-please tell me this is a joke, Katherine. I said.

I bitterly rubbed the palm of my hands against my head and then rubbed it down my face [Ba –Bum]; my chest would not stop pounding.

I apologize, I'm repentant!

Katherine looked at me, and the color of my cheeks started turning slightly red, I could feel the warmness.

"Are you okay?"

No, I am not! You said that you would stay as long as I loved you. I still love you more than ever. You are the air that I breathe.

"If that were true, you would have never cheated. I am moving on, and I recommend that you do the same. I cannot do this anymore. I cannot think. I cannot concentrate on my schoolwork. My grades are – my mind is slipping. It's over!"

Katherine, it's called love; it does that to some people. Just forgive me and let's get through this. I love you; I can't – let go. I am not giving up."

"Jason, our separation does not have to be this hard. If you love me, you will let me go."

Katherine, if you love me, you would stay.

"But I can't!"

You cannot, or you will not?

"I will not."

Ba-Bum, Jason's heart pounds faster against his chest. Katherine, why are you so cold-hearted?

Katherine –

I knew if I lightened up, I would fall weak. Just like he told me, "If you beat the barrier hard enough; it would break." Pl-please leave! I said.

"Well – Katherine, I will respect you and your Wishes. I will back off just for a little while. However, I promise I will never stop loving you! I will never stop calling you! I will never stop speaking to you!"

I was thinking, please don't ever let go.

Jason –

I wiped away her tears. Then kissed her cheek and closed the door. We were hurting severely.

I knew that her education meant everything to her. There-fore, I left.

Katherine –

I began crying, buckets of tears. My heart was broken. How-ever, I knew I needed to walk away.

Jason –

I was mighty, but even the most influential men fall weak for love and plummet.

CHAPTER 10

K atherine –

Things still were not as simple as I imagined, a matter of fact, the separation seemed more complicated. Jason continued to come to my recitals, and he sat in the front row as usual.

Marcy was sitting next to him; her baby bump was showing just a tiny bit. She looked at me with this gloating smile. She was glowing.

Jason clapped his hands the loudest. Maybe he was reminiscing on how things used to be.

The next week, he came again alone, after the recital was over, Jason reached his hand towards me. My body brushed against his hand as I walked past him.

It was the hardest thing ever, desiring to stay, but forced to walk away because of your dreams – because of his mistakes. I never looked up, nor back.

My heart and soul were aching. There were plenty of days when I felt as if I could not make it without Jason. My life was depressing.

I needed him! I haven't had a decent night of sleep since our breakup.

I try to fight the feelings, but my love for him kept slapping me in the face. The pain, the heartaches, the headaches, the tears, the dreams, the feelings! Would not go away, and no man could suffice?"

Katie –

Jason kept asking me, "Have Katherine asked about me?" Déjà vu I heard the same question from Katherine. No matter how brave Katherine was pretending to be, it was entirely the opposite; her heart shattered.

However, she made me promise not to say a word of it to Jason. Katherine was purposely avoiding him; she was stepping back from the relationship. However, he was standing in front of her marching forward.

Jason desired more than a friendship, but at the time that was all that she was offering. Katherine could not handle falling deeper in love with him.

However, Jason would not leave her alone. He called her three times a day, every day; he needed to hear her sweet sexy voice. However, Katherine was ignoring his phone calls.

I remember when Katherine and Jason reunited. It was wonderful.

Katherine –

I created a perception and the direction which I wanted my life to go. I had it all planned out, and love was never in my plans until I met Jason.

He was interfering with my views. Day by day, I saw the endless agony in Jason's eyes. I wanted to reach out to him. I wanted to apologize. I ached to comfort him. However, I had to stay active.

I felt something special when he was around, my heart rate thumped swifter, and no matter how much I avoided him, I could not run from love, it kept stalking me.

Jason came into my life at the spur of the moment. Even though I had a brief encounter with love; it was not going to flatter me away from my dreams. He wasn't going to hurt me again.

Miss. Roosevelt, I called myself as I smiled and played around in the mirror. I was the reflection of my mother.

However, since the prom was over, my life – my happiness was over; it was time to reach my goals – face reality.

I graduated with honors. I worked hard, and I earned the highest GPA in school. I was the first African American young person to graduate as valedictorian at the school.

That was just the beginning of my life and what an accomplishment – I had a purpose; it was to become successful, and my peers nominated me as most likely to succeed. I seemed to satisfy everyone, but Jason and me.

Graduation day was the second-best moment of my life, but it was not my first triumph! Dancing with Jason was the first magnificent sparkle, the glimmer in my eye.

I posted in my journal: "Dear world – I did it! I did it! I beat the odds, and I have survived the impossible. I deserved a standing ovation, and I got one."

Then life punched me in the face just like the pregnancy. Life defeated me!

Excitedly, —

I began applying to some of the best colleges in Washington, D.C., and they accepted me at the Bright's University of Maryland.

However, my parents were a little skeptical about me venturing out on my own. My father, Paul Roosevelt, was not ready for his princess to leave the castle.

However, his princess was ready to become a Queen. My father wasn't a sympathetic king; he was more like a knight guarding the fortress. However, he could not sweet-talk me into staying.

Despite all our disagreements about what was best for me, he always made me feel safe and loved beyond measures. It was a special bond between us.

Father told me that he was pleased with me. He said if I ever needed anything, to talk, cry, or yell, it did not matter what time it was; he was only a phone call away.

He handed me the keys to my very own apartment and car. I ran and screamed with excitement! I was crying and packed with joy! I slammed my lips against his' cheek.

I had finally become an adult, and another dream had come true, and why, because I never stopped dreaming, just as my mother said.

When I walked into the apartment for the first time, I felt free, and it was the most significant feeling ever. I was able to do whatever I wanted with whomever I wanted! However, I was an adult but single.

Katie –

We were inseparable; we did everything together: went to the movies, sports events, and parties.

We met up at the mall to eat lunch at the restaurant for the last time. When we saw each other, we boohooed, hugged and kissed, we were happy for one another yet sad.

Our friendship had grown over the years; we never spent one day apart. When we finished eating our lunches, we went our separate ways.

Maryann left Washington D.C. to start her college classes. Walter, Jason, and I enrolled at a local University. Katherine desired to take some business classes; therefore, she went to a college three hundred miles from her hometown. That school offered her the best opportunities to expand her education.

Jason was still angry over the breakup; although he loved Katherine totally, he could not accept her conditions. He could not pretend as if love never existed, not as well as Katherine could.

Katherine was weary and disappointed. She was ready for love; however, the one person who she treasured the most had moved on, and he forced her to do the same.

Time had drawn them together; now, it was tearing them

apart. Jason and Katherine started their college classes; they were so busy doing their schoolwork that they never had time for one another.

CHAPTER 11

E ventually, Katherine applied for a clerical position at the Northeastern Oil & Gas Corporation. She had seen a flyer on the college bulletin board.

Mr. Taylor offered young women and men an opportunity to earn extra money while they attended college. Taylor's Northeastern Oil & Gas Corporation was an African American-owned company, directed by the Taylor family at least that is what the flyer said.

Jason's last name was Taylor. Katherine wondered if the owner of the business was kin to him. However, Jason did not appear to be a billionaire.

Katherine applied for the position. Then she called Katie; she knew that if anyone had the answers to her questions, it would be her.

Katie answered the phone. She was excited to hear from Katherine; they hadn't spoken in weeks. She asked Katherine, "How is the relationship?"

Katherine changed the subject; she asked Katie if Jason was kin to the owner of the company. Although Katie knew the truth, she told Katherine, "I will have to ask Walter and call you back later."

Katie never mentioned that Jason's father owned the company, and Jason was the heir. Walter told Katie about Jason's riches, but he made her promise that she would not say a word of it to Katherine.

Jason was working hard trying to create a future for them,

yes, he was busy, but he was doing it all for Katherine, he wanted to give her everything that she ever wanted.

Katie knew that Katherine was avoiding her question; how her relationship with Thomas was. Katie thought Katherine was acting a little peculiar.

It seemed odd that she wasn't willing to discuss her relationship. Katherine was an opened person; she didn't keep many secrets.

However, Katherine did not want to say that Thomas was beating her. It was six months before graduation; Katherine received a phone call from Northeastern Oil & Gas Corporation.

"May I speak with Katherine Roosevelt?"

"Yes, this is she? How can I help you?"

"My name is Elizabeth; I am the secretary for Northeastern Oil & Gas Corporation. I am calling you to inform you that the position that you applied for belonged to you if you are still interested.

"Yes!"

"I know this is concise notice, but can you come in tomorrow?"

"Yes!"

"I will see you then."

Katherine walked into the office; she had on a black and red pinstripe suit with a red blouse and shoes. She walked up to the receptionist.

"May I speak with Elizabeth?"

"May I have your name?"

"Katherine Roosevelt."

"She's expecting you."

The receptionist took Katherine down a long hallway and sat her in an oversized, beautiful office. She asked Katherine to take a seat and wait for Mr. Taylor in his office.

Katherine sat in the chair; she looked all around. Lots of different pictures were hanging on the walls. Some of the photographs were sitting on the desk; they were everywhere.

She looked closer, and then she noticed pictures of Walter,

Katie, and Maryann hanging on the wall. Katherine stood up and walked around.

She saw more pictures of Jason and her sitting on the desk; it was the pictures from the prom. She begins wondering, "Why Mr. Taylor had so many pictures of them in his office? Who was he?"

Then the door opened, she turned completely around; Katherine looked up, and then she saw his face. He stole her breath away.

"What a small world," she said. It was Jason.

"Have a seat," said Jason as he sat down as well.

"What are you doing here?"

Jason hesitated. "This is my father, Theodore Taylor's company, and I am the heir."

"I never knew that."

"Because I never mentioned it," he grinned.

"If you would've known the truth, Katherine, that I was the owner of the company, would you still have applied for the position?"

"Certainly; it didn't matter who worked here; I was looking for a career."

"What about a man?"

"No, I have one. You should be more concerned about Marcy and your baby." Jason stares at her, and she stares back.

"Marcy miscarried, and we ended up splitting up. I was with her because of the baby, nothing more."

"I am sorry to hear that! However, are you offering me the job?"

"I am offering you that and more."

"I don't think Thomas would like that."

"Who is Thomas, and what about – what I like"?

Katherine hesitated, "Hmmm Interesting! What about – what you like? I am still livid! You liked Marcy remember?"

"Sexually, I did; however, I acknowledge that I made a mistake."

Jason stared at Katherine and asked, "Your boyfriend? I –

thought, never mind. I can offer Thomas a position too. Jason chuckled. "When can you start or when can he start?"

Katherine said, "You're not funny, not at all, and I can start immediately."

"Can you come in tomorrow?" She nodded.

Jason said, "What happened to us?"

"You tell me! You stopped caring and calling!"

"Is that what you recall?"

"Yes, and the pain kept leaving and coming."

"So, did mines! Yes, I did stop calling, but please understand; I was incredibly busy with work and school after you dumped me. Just as you, I was securing a great life; however, not just for me, but for you as well."

"I wanted you to have – I wanted to give you all the things that you ever desired in life. I didn't want to deprive you of anything because I couldn't afford it. I knew we would cross paths again. That's how fate works! I did not stop caring Katherine; we vowed never to stop loving one another. Remember! I was drying you off after you fell into the lake, and you said," "I will never stop loving you." "So, ask yourself, what happened to us?"

"I did not fall, you pushed me into the water, and sometimes vows are meant to be broken."

"What? Are you referring to your vows? Katherine, vows are not meant to be broken – ever! So, wouldn't you agree that words are merely insignificant words?"

"Are they?" Jason, I appreciate the job opportunity, but I am happy with Thomas."

"There goes them magnificent words again. You love breaking my heart! Are you pleased?"

"Yes, I am thrilled, and I have to go."

"Sure, you do! One thing that you are good at is running away from your feelings."

Katherine had to walk away quickly because she wasn't entirely over Jason, and she didn't want him to see the pain that was in her eyes.

When she saw him again, the ache that she felt over the

months finally disappeared. Katherine's life was terrific now; she had reunited with the love of her life.

Everything that she desired was right there in her perfect world! However, she was missing the last piece of the puzzle, and no matter how hard she tried to fit another piece in, it would not pair.

She could not pretend as if Jason did not exist, but she was willing to work on it. Jason thought Katherine was still as beautiful as the first day they met; he was in love all over again.

Jason –

I was not worried about a career because my father had started preparing me to take over the family business since I was the age of twelve. Our family had more money than we could count.

I was managing college classes and making business decisions; I did not have time for a woman. I was trying to create a future for Katherine and me.

I was working hard – so hard that I did not notice that I had abandoned Katherine until she was not there anymore. However, I never stopped loving her.

Then we begin interviewing people for a clerical position; I received a batch of applications. I was scanning through the submissions. After reviewing dozens of bids, I noticed that Katherine Roosevelt had applied for the job as well.

I didn't expect ever to see Katherine again. The Katherine Roosevelt that I grew to love, and I danced with at the prom.

I was not willing to let her go that easily, never again. I was going to offer her the opportunity to prove herself worthy of the job and my heart. Besides, if she worked for me, it would be easier to fit her into my hectic schedule.

There were hundreds of applications of well-qualified applicants, but Katherine was the only person who could fill the position in my heart. However, I was not aware that she was already in a relationship, which she had previously stolen someone else's heart, or someone had taken hers'.

Katherine had broken my heart time and time again! I had to win her back, she was a rare diamond, and her sparkler was blinding my vision and my heart. She did not seem to have any faults; she was flawless.

Katherine was not an alternative in my life; she was a priority. I had found the beautiful woman of my dreams, and I didn't only see her while I slept. I saw her when I was awake, as well. She was not just a dream; she was real.

She was an ambitious, eye-catching executive who wore pin-stripe suits with her hair styled in a bun. Katherine was classy with a fantastic smile. She won my heart! When she walked into the conference room for the meetings, she enchanted the business world with her prominent projects.

I was proud to walk beside her; I knew she would be the perfect wife if she weren't dating Thomas, and I was patiently waiting for him to make a mistake so that I could take her away from him.

Later, I promoted Katherine for her resilient leadership skills and wise investing. Katherine was a great asset to the company. I was lovesick over her. I needed Katherine in my life forever and a day.

◆ ◆ ◆

Katherine –

Well, back to my present story. Early that next morning, I woke up and got ready for work.

I cheerfully walked into my office, expecting to find Jason sitting in my chair again. I opened the door with a big smile on my face and busted into the room like "I am here!"

But he was not there; disheartened, my soul dropped to the floor. Then the office door opened; I smiled and turned around to greet Jason.

I was troubled; it was Thomas. What was Thomas doing here, did he follow me?

I said, "Good morning, what brought you this way." He replied, "I stopped by to say good morning." He must have noticed the disappointment on my face because he asked me, "Were you expecting someone else, perhaps Jason?" I knew if I told the truth; he would kill me.

I frowned and replied, "No, I wasn't." Why would I be expecting Jason? But I was hoping to see him. I kissed Thomas on the cheek. Thomas must have felt insulted by the kiss!

He grabbed my neck tightly and pulled me toward him. I flinched! He kissed my lips. I was afraid of him, and I willingly returned the kiss.

Thomas left my office laughing and mocking me. "No, I wasn't expecting anyone else." He smiled. He knew I was expecting Jason.

But Thomas had planted so much fear into me that I would never admit that to him. Although I was afraid, my heart was committed to Jason.

Again, that was the only thing that Thomas couldn't control. I was confused, going from one man to the other. No one ever knew my secrets; I was able to keep my composure despite what was going on.

I kept smiling, although I was heartbroken. I needed someone to notice my pain and rescue me. But how could they read my heart? I never shed a tear, at least not openly.

I walked around with a transparent glass window in front of my face, looking out, enjoying everyone else's happiness. How sad!

My relationship was discreet, and there were so many things going on in my life that were unspoken. I was embarrassed; I was not ready to reveal the truth.

My body masked by cuts, scars, hidden welts, and open wounds that would not heal. The size of them was increasing day-by-day.

What happened to that perfect life that I planned? The idea that I had envisioned was just another hallucination. My dreams and hopes were dead.

Everything in my world was complete, but now, sadness had taken over, and it was heart-breaking. I started enjoying sitting in dark corners and being alone.

I hated the sunshine; it was bright and sparkling, and I needed total darkness. My life had become – dim.

When it rained, I sat on the hard metal bench in the backyard. I was mesmerized by the rain.

Drip, Drip, Drip, but it was not enough; my tears were flowing rapidly, and I needed the rain to pour and wash them away. It's funny how quickly my life had changed.

I wasn't the typical girl next door. I consider myself to be one of the Joneses.

But my life was empty. Jason and I had more money than we ever needed, but it couldn't buy back my happiness or my peace of mind. Money could not take away my pain, and it couldn't salvage my sanity.

I was smart, I had an answer for everything, yet I couldn't explain why I was staying in an abusive relationship. Was I crazier than Thomas? I sat down and deliberated. "Why?"

The same blank answer kept appearing. Maybe, it was the fear that a man could never love a wounded woman.

While men and women were fighting for the country's freedom, I was struggling for liberty in my home. The doors open, I cringe, and I'm startled.

Thomas yells my name, and I am frightened. I'm always wondering if he's going to hit me today or will it be tomorrow? Who's going to fight for me and my freedom?

What hurts me the most is, I go outside, and no one sees my trauma. No one considers the long sleeves that I wear in the summer or the long pants that cover my legs.

I'm ashamed of the marks that cover me, and not one person asks why you are wearing those clothes. It's hot outside.

They would rather believe I'm weird, and maybe I think you are bizarre for being so happy all the time; besides, who giggles all day long. I was angry with the world and mostly with myself.

I guess I am strange for living in an unhealthy relationship.

Or maybe I'm a hero to bear such discomfort and never come forward.

Some women bump their toes and rush to the emergency room. I get a fist to the eye, and I cover it with make-up. I am so depressed and confused.

Domestic violence and dominance had taken control of my life, and I was searching for a way out. I had cut my wrists many times, silently; I stood in front of the upstairs window. I was a step away from jumping out.

I was building up the courage for that day. But the scars that ached most were inside, and those were the hardest to heal. I wanted the relationship to end, and my escape was crucial. But I could not get away from Thomas, and he would not let me go.

I was bottled-up and enslaved by his obsessions and fascinations. I was swinging by the thread, and Thomas held the scissors.

Jason –

Astounded! — was the word which described my feelings as I watched Katherine and Thomas through my slightly opened office blinds? I could not believe what I witnessed through my window.

Thomas grabbed Katherine by the neck and then pulled her toward him as if she was his pet? Katherine, trembling! She never looked around; she didn't see me watching her; she was too frightened to blink or take her eyes off Thomas.

I stood inside my cold office, pacing back and forth. Although it was freezing, I had to take off my jacket; it was becoming slightly warm.

My first reaction was to race out of my office and break Thomas' arm into pieces; I was infuriated. But I was more upset that Katherine didn't trust me as a friend or a boss.

I knew from Thomas' actions that there was more going on in the relationship than Katherine was portraying. No man could be that brave or comfortable with grabbing a woman by the neck inside of an open public building unless it had happened before.

I cried; Katherine and the whole ordeal broke my heart. The fear that I saw in her eyes – I knew she was petrified, and it showed. But I stayed inside of my office; I didn't want to embarrass or harm her. So,

I kept her secret hidden. But I could not guarantee her or Thomas that I wouldn't react the next time.

Katherine –

Later that day, I made plans to have lunch with Samantha, Brittany, Maryann, and Katie. We met at a small café across the street from the job; we were sitting around the table eating sandwiches and soup, drinking tea, laughing and chitchatting about our lives.

We were talking about both the incredible and the regretful days, reminiscing about our teenage years. Then Samantha asked the question – how things between Thomas and me were.

I began picturing Thomas slapping, hitting and kicking me. I stared at Samantha for a moment, wondering how I should answer this question. Then I lied and uttered, "Great." But I held back my tears.

My relationship had flashed before me again. A tear fell, I wiped it quickly, and I immediately changed the subject. "I have an annoying life," I said, smiling. "We are here to have fun! I need a glass of wine; anyone else wants one?

They were looking at each other. Then Samantha asked me if everything was okay, "It's marvelous," I replied. I needed to leave; I got up and kissed everyone goodbye.

I went home. I couldn't spend another second pretending to be happy.

I was humiliated! I couldn't tell my family, friends, or Jason, that I was living a terrifying secret life. Thomas was restraining me, and he was violent. If someone – anyone would lift my clothing, they would see the scars.

Even the dark ones were starting to surface; I was falling apart. Samantha was a music teacher and my oldest sister. She was married to Jeffery White, who was the principal at the school where she worked.

Brittany was my youngest sister; she was a seamstress, and she was single. "I am not ready for love," Brittany said. She was always looking for a party.

Before I left the cafe, my sisters and I joked about our father, who did not condone sex before marriage. He disapproved of my relationship with Thomas.

Jason was one of the reasons I wanted to wait; then, he cheated. I was angry, lonely, and I realized that I moved too quickly, now look at me trapped in Thomas obsessive world.

I always desired to make my father proud of me. He saw something in Thomas that I overlooked.

But Thomas was my first tangible relationship. I loved the attentiveness, although it was the wrong type of attention.

My father had always told me when there was nothing else to believe in, look towards the sky. But I couldn't pray, because my sky was no longer blue.

It was cloudy just like my life – the life that I wanted to end; because I didn't want to spend another wasteful second in Thomas' tarnished arms. But, as much as I hated him, there was that insane part of me that cared. Although he harmed me, part of me didn't want to hurt him.

Was I crazy? How could I care for a man who continued to abuse me with no sympathy? Or was I immune to pain? I secretly wanted Thomas to change since he wasn't that controlling or abusive when we first met.

He was a great man with a loving heart. So, I thought! He opened the doors and carried my books during and after school. He bought me expensive gifts (flowers, dinner, and lingerie, etc.).

It seemed like a healthy relationship. But what changed Thomas? Maybe it was me, the clothing that I wore, or the late hours that I worked.

Perhaps if I loved Thomas as much as I enjoyed myself or Jason, I would understand his obsession. Maybe the real problem was me.

If I didn't provoke him, he wouldn't hit or rape me, would he? At least, that's what I started telling myself. I must've done something wrong–If I would've just obeyed.

Maybe I gave too much of my time to my family and friends? My entire life was an "if or maybe."

I knew no one could empathize with him if they knew the truth. That thin line was getting smaller. I was beginning to drift more and more toward hating Thomas, but I was holding on by compassion.

What would be my next move? Would I stay and continue to live a lie, or leave and admit my relationship was disintegrating?

Did I say, "I can't acknowledge? Was that my dilemma — I'm in denial? A simple answer to the question, but, to me, the answer wasn't that simple.

The next morning around 10:30 am, Jason, and I greeted one another in the hallway. While we were talking, Thomas appeared suddenly. In a jealous frenzy, he walked up to me and shoved me against the wall.

I was terrified! He asked me boldly, "What's going on? Is this a private meeting? Katherine, are you having sex with him?"

I opened my mouth to speak, but as usual, before I could respond, Thomas abruptly interrupted me. He insisted on talking to me in the office promptly and privately.

But I knew that would be a mistake. I refused to leave with Thomas and put myself in a dangerous situation. Since I appeared to be uneasy and reluctant; Jason walked up to me and asked: "if everything was okay."

Thomas said, "Are you the hero?"

Jason ignored him. "Katherine, are you okay?"

I tried to make my Yes sound sincere.

Jason whispered, "I can protect you."

I murmured, "What?"

"I can protect you."

"Shut up, Thomas yelled!"

I was baffled; I pondered, does he know, but that was impossible. I had kept my secret well hidden.

Jason reached out his hand. "You don't have to live like this." But Thomas pushed his hands away.

"Are you the white knight?"

Jason said, "Leave my building."

He turned abruptly and left the building. But he winked his eye as he retreated. I knew he was steaming. "I'll see you at the house," he told me.

I was afraid; I always knew what that meant. I had to escape after Thomas left the building; I began yelling at Jason.

"How could you jeopardize my life and my relationship?"

Jason shouted back, "There is no relationship, Katherine, there IS no relationship. I saw that piece of crap grab you by the neck. A person who truly loves you would never touch you in such a violent manner."

How do you know about real love? I haven't seen any women come through this door." Jason was suddenly silent. "I am waiting for an answer?" I loved Jason, but I was fighting my thoughts.

"How long has Thomas been hitting you?" Teardrops began to fall.

"You need to move on."

"I haven't. I won't."

Jason wiped the tears away with his thumb. I was speechless, and I denied everything, but I was willing to listen to him. I knew he was speaking out of love, but the real words were the way he stared at me.

Jason leaned over and kissed my lips softly. "Please allow me to attest my love for you."

Katherine hesitated. "I love you, but I am obligated to my relationship. I have a responsibility."

Jason yelled. "RE-SPON-SI-BIL-I-TY? You have a responsibility to Yourself; you owe yourself a better life. Look at you, blaming me for protecting you and, yet, you are taking the side of a man that abuses you.

I am not a psychiatrist, but I don't need to be to figure out there is a problem; and I can't help you until you help yourself."

I turned my face toward the ceiling. I don't need any help.

"Take off the makeup, take off that jacket."

I don't have to take this; I am leaving. I said.

"I'm only trying to help you."

I don't need any fucking help. Now leave me alone, I am out of here. I yelled.

Although I knew it wasn't right for Thomas to hit me, I felt like it wasn't right for me to abandon him either. My life was in turmoil.

Jason whispered, "Don't go, you are a precious diamond, and your happiness is worth more than my billions of dollars, my company, my home, my cars, and my pride."

No man had ever said that to me. Your billions of dollars, I repeated numbly.

"Maybe not the money," he laughed; "but I can make you smile just like that every single day if you give me a chance."

Jason, I must leave. I left from work in a hurry. I was trying to figure out what needed to be done to keep Thomas composed.

When I arrived home; I saw the car parked in the driveway. I got out of the car and walked up to the front door. Before I could open the door, Thomas came out and pushed the door into my body, and I fell to the concrete driveway. My purse fell on the ground.

Then Thomas sat on top of me and began hitting me with his fist violently. I screamed, but he kept beating me. Then he raped me outside in the yard as if I was rubbish.

My house was so far from my neighbor's that no one heard me yell. I lay on the ground and cried.

What did I do to deserve this? At that moment I realized 'there is no way out.' Thomas wasn't going to change; I was holding onto the one dream that was not going to come true.

However, that last forceful punch set me free. I knew at that moment – that very moment I realized that I needed to leave, or

I was going die by Thomas' hands.

I looked at myself, my clothing, "I went from riches to rags. While I lay on the ground bleeding, I realized now was not the time to give up.

But I was tired of living in fear, going to the doctor to be stitched up, and being miserable. If I were going to die, it would be in my own hands.

When Thomas finally freed me; I grabbed my purse from the driveway and raced to the car, my heels were slipping on the wet grass. I scratched my leg on a branch outside trying to get to safety. I kept looking back to see if Thomas was behind me.

I hopped into the car and drove until I found that spot to end it all. Then I saw the giant sign for Seashore Beach. It was dark, private, and no one was around.

Despite the warnings that said, "no vehicles allowed beyond this point," I parked the car on the beach sand. I looked at the water; the waves were calm and peaceful just as I desired to be.

I left everything inside the car, including my purse. I opened the door. I ran and ran until I reached the edge of the water.

Then I walked closer towards the water. The waves were moving forward and then drifting backward.

I stood there for a while watching the water. I could smell the scent of the ocean.

I felt the gritty sand between my toes. The rippling water was freezing as it splashed across my feet. But I just wanted to be free; I wanted the pain to stop. I walked deeper into the water. I didn't want to kill myself, but there was no other way out.

I was tired, hungry, and I wanted to rest. I heard my phone ringing. I ignored the ringing phone and kept walking towards the immense ocean. But the person would not hang up.

I kept walking more in-depth into the water, but the caller refused to hang up. The phone kept ringing and ringing. It was annoying, and I wanted a peaceful death. I went to the car to turn off the ringer, and I noticed it was Jason.

I couldn't turn the phone off, nor could I walk away; I stood there and stared at the phone and then I sighed. I stayed still, and then I thought to myself, "The knight protecting his castle."

I dropped the phone in the dirt and walked back into the water — step by step, deeper and deeper. The cold water splashed against my chest. But Jason wouldn't give up. He kept calling me persistently. I kept ignoring the ringing phone.

I kept walking until the cold water covered my breast and smashed violently against my chest. But Jason still would not give up.

I took more steps forward until the water covered my head, and the waves bounced me about, my head was bobbing, I was sinking.

My hair floated with the ripping tides. My heart was hammering against my chest, ba-bum, ba-bum, ba-bum. I swallowed mouthfuls of water, but it wasn't like holding my head under the water in the tub; it was much different, saltier.

I kept hearing Jason's voice in my ear, whispering, "I love you!" The ringing stopped, so did I? He cut the core of my lifeline. I needed to hear that sound again—the sound of my phone ringing.

I swam up above the water, and the cold waves took me under again. I tried again, and I sank back into the ocean. I didn't have the strength nor oxygen to fight, but the silence made the struggle even harder.

The disconnection from Jason forced me into a different survival mode. I wasn't going to die in this water. I wasn't going to die without Jason.

The love that I felt for Jason wouldn't allow me to stay under the water. I was coughing and struggling to breathe. Although Thomas was the reason I wanted to die, Jason was my purpose for living.

With all my might and power, I swam, and I swam until I reached the shore. I don't know how long I rested on the gritty sand. Finally, I crawled and then picked up my phone.

WHAT? What do you want? My virginity, I no longer have that because Thomas stole it from me. What could I possibly offer you?

My scars: which one would you like, the one on my wrist, the one on my eye or the one in my heart? Leave me alone! I want it to end so I can die peacefully.

Jason said, "I can offer you the world and do whatever it takes to give it to you. But I cannot let you die because my heart would die. I will die, and I am not ready to die, not yet! So, no, I will not leave you alone."

He paused. "What I want from you is to give you the love that you deserve. I want to touch you the way you need to be touched, and I want to protect you how you deserved to be protected. If a little sex comes with that; it's okay too." She laughed.

You always knew how to do that!

"What?"

Make me smile!

Cold, hungry, tired, and lonely! I finally gave in and told Jason where I was. Jason begged me to wait for him and then five minutes later, he arrived.

"That was quick."

"I have been searching for you for an hour," he shouted, "How could you let him harm you like this?"

"Do you think I wanted this?"

Jason rubbed his hands across my face and began apologizing for abandoning me. How funny. If it was possible, he cared about my safety more than I.

"As long as I live, Thomas will never hit you again, but you have to allow me to protect you."

He turned his back to me.

"Take off your wet clothes."

Jason took off his shirt and gave it to me. Put this on. I stared at his bareback. After I was done changing, Jason picked up my clothes from the ground; he kissed me and carried me to his car.

He opened his car door and then sat me down carefully. He put the keys into the ignition, kissed me on the lips, and then gave me the address of his house.

"I will follow you to make sure that idiot doesn't cut you off."

I drove off, and Jason followed me. I was frightened and con-templating if I should stay or go.

What would happen if I didn't return home soon? Spontan-eously, I stopped in the middle of the road. Jason came to the car. I demanded, "Take me back home right now," but he re-fused.

I arrived at the address, and it was a mansion. The house was large and beautiful. Jason got out of my car and opened the gate with the remote control.

Then I drove down the long path; it seemed like it took me forever to reach the house. When we went inside, Jason picked up the telephone to call the police, but I hung it up.

I was afraid of Thomas or what he may do. He was a so-called distinguished attorney who knew over half of the officers in the precinct. He probably wouldn't even be charged.

Besides, I didn't want to ruin his high reputation.

January 12, 2011

Jason called my parents over; I'd never told them anything about Jason since the prom; they had no clue that he was my boss. My parents came to Jason's house with the intentions of taking me home. They rang the doorbell; Jason went to the door and opened it.

When my mother saw him, she noticed that he was the same Jason that danced with me at the prom. I heard her ask him, "Where is she?"

Jason led them to the bedroom; my bruises shook my mother and father. Then Mom started crying and asked me, "Who did this?" But I wouldn't say a word.

Then Jason blurted out, "Thomas." My parents insisted that they take me to the hospital to get me checked out. But, again, I refused help.

"No," I yelled.

Mother asked me, "what happened; Why?"

She had tears in her eyes. I paused. I tried to be resilient! But my mother's eyes were filled with more tears; she was in much pain. I broke down, sobbing.

It was uncontrollable. After Jason blurred out, "Thomas hit her;" I confessed the truth to my mother. Thomas had beat me and then raped me. I couldn't tell Jason that I was raped that night.

Yet, I was angry with Jason for revealing my secret. I wanted to escape Thomas, and I tried to explain to my father and friends, but, I couldn't because I didn't want to let all of them down.

Mother was outraged, and she said, "I brought you into this world, and I never put one bruise on you, and he beats you like this. Oh, my goodness, Katherine, you kept all of this to yourself. Why didn't you tell me much sooner? How long have you been keeping all these secrets? The abuse, the medication, what else are you keeping from me? I am disappointed because you didn't come to me sooner."

I quickly realized that all my skeletons were starting to come out of the closet; the refuge that I had built around them was crumbling down. More tears start flowing from my eyes.

I don't know. I stopped keeping track after the twentieth beating or more.

Mother started to cry again. She hugged me and said: "Why didn't you tell me?" I said, "I was too ashamed, especially when he raped me."

"Raped you?" Mother fell apart, "Let me tell you my story," mother said.

Her dad crumpled: "I'm sorry, Katherine."

"Why? You didn't do anything?"

He said, "No, I didn't! I didn't protect you. I didn't forewarn you; I didn't prepare you, and I didn't see the warning signs. I didn't question you more about the pills when your mother told me."

"Mum told you?"

"Yes!"

My father wanted to kill Thomas. Jason told him to take his

gun. But Father wasn't a killer, and as much as he wished he could, he didn't honor violence. He placed all his worries in the hands of God. I should have.

When they left, Jason carried me to the bathroom to bathe me, and after he finished, he rested alongside me. He held me all night.

Lying in his arms was pleasing; Thomas never made me feel loved. That reflection and sparkle that I was searching for, I had found it in Jason's eyes.

Jason's touch left me breathless; I had never felt such incredible emotions before. But I didn't want to rush into another relationship so suddenly, mainly because I was still in the first one.

But Thomas' problems were increasing. Because I didn't care about his feelings anymore or my responsibilities. I didn't care about the stupid mistakes that I had made.

What I cared about was being wrapped in Jason's arms. I didn't want to return home; I was already there. I was where I belonged, the place which I had been longing for, I had found it.

Thomas –

I stopped by Katherine's job; she and Jason were standing in the hallway, talking and laughing. I was infuriated!

First, they disrespected me at the Christmas party; now they were alone in the hall having fun again. I reacted; I walked up to her and pushed her against the wall.

I wanted to scare her into telling me the truth, and I wanted to make sure this would never happen again. The muscles in my face tightened.

She was frightened; her pupils dilated, I asked her what was going on.

I wanted to talk to her alone in her office so that we could talk about things like rational adults, but she refused, which made me more upset.

Then Jason kept disrupting us. Who was he to tell me what to do with my woman? I wanted to close his mouth for good, but security was a phone call away.

Jason, this is not your business, I said, but he wasn't listening or understanding me. Katherine was my lady, but he wanted to be her 'hero.'

I supposed he imagined he loved her more than I, but I would die first before handing her over to him. I lifted my shirt to expose my gun. I suppose the boy thought I was afraid to use it. His threats didn't scare me, but it wasn't the right time to confront him.

Jason asked me to leave his building, and I did. I winked my eye at Katherine and walked away.

She knew what would happen when she came home, and when Katherine arrived, I was boiling in rage.

I slammed the door into her face. She had brought this on herself, and it was all her fault. She provoked me to anger. I beat her and then raped her.

She screamed, but I didn't care! I enjoyed beating fear into her; besides no one could hear her cries.

I became exhausted, and I let go of her; maybe she learned her lesson now. It's possible that a good beating would influence her next decision.

Perhaps the next time she would obey me. I lay on the couch. She stormed down the driveway, but I didn't care.

She had left home before; however, she always returned home. Later that night, I woke up to check on Katherine, but I couldn't find her anywhere.

I searched outside, but the car was gone. I knew she was with Jason, but I didn't know where he lived. I called her phone, and she didn't answer.

I left a message on her phone; she was going to die if she didn't get home immediately. I couldn't live without her, nor could I watch her live a great life without me.

I had to find her. But how would I explain this to her parents? I had to go over there to see if they had seen her.

I waited a few hours, and then I knocked on the door, and Mrs.

Roosevelt answered. She began asking me too many questions that I couldn't answer.

Then she called Mr. Roosevelt to the door. They kept questioning me, "Why would she leave?" But I couldn't tell them the truth; I had beaten and raped her.

Mr. Roosevelt called Katherine's phone, but she did not answer. They questioned me again.

"Why would she leave," Mrs. Roosevelt asked?

I became aggravated by all the questions, and I told them, "I do not know where she is; as I said earlier when I woke up, she was gone."

"Maybe she's with her boss, Jason," I said with innuendo. I was trying to figure out if Katherine had told her parents anything about him.

"Why would she be with him?" her father asked me.

I replied, "She didn't tell you that she was cheating on me with him?"

Mr. Roosevelt yelled, "What? Are you insinuating that my daughter is a cheater; because I did not raise Katherine to be that way and if she is with Jason, I am sure she has good reasons? I would force you out of my house, but I need you to explain why my daughter would just leave for no reason?"

I almost forgot Mr. Roosevelt was an older man; I wanted to punch him just like I hit his daughter. Then Mrs. Roosevelt said, "Let's call the police."

Although I genuinely believed they knew where Katherine was, I wasn't willing to call their bluff.

I told Mrs. Roosevelt, "There is no need to do that, I'm convinced she will return home. I rushed to the door, and I asked them to give me a call if they heard from Katherine.

I knew Katherine wouldn't tell anyone what I had done; I beat her plenty of times before, and she had never said a word. I kept calling her cell phone, but she still wouldn't answer.

CHAPTER 12

Thomas –

     I went to Katherine's job site to see if she was there. The secretary told me that she hadn't heard from her. I left the office more frustrated than ever.

I was wondering where Katherine and Jason were. I had sworn to kill them once I found them.

My love for Katherine became an addiction. I felt lifeless without her; I was desperate to see her, driven by desire. My love for Katherine was turning into something that I could no longer control.

I could not concentrate on my job or my kid. Every day that I spent with Katherine felt like our very first date. Was I delusional?

No matter who I was with, or where I was, if Katherine called, I came. I never missed a day without speaking to her; the separation was killing me.

If she would just come back, I wouldn't be upset, but she was ignoring me, and that was sending me into a crazy rage.

Jason –

I knew the truth, but I wanted to hear it from Katherine's mouth. When he slammed her into the wall, I didn't defend her right way; I wanted to know how long she was going to lie to me.

But, I finally had enough, and then I asked Katherine if she was okay. Thomas leered me.

"Katherine is my business and my property; are you her

hero?"

Well, the word property didn't sit well with me; I had a problem with that word; it offended me.

I said, Yes, I am her hero, and Katherine cannot be bought with a price tag nor sold with one. She is not a slave; those days are long over.

"Mind your business and walk away quickly before things become unpleasant."

I replied. First, Katherine is my business and secondly, what's on your mind?

Thomas lifted his shirt to expose his gun. But I wasn't afraid; if gunplay was what he wanted, then gunplay is what he would get. He wasn't going to bully me.

You better do more than show it, you better be willing to use it, and if you don't kill me; you will regret pointing that gun at me. Furthermore, this is my building. I'm not asking; I'm demanding that you leave, and since your lady works for me, she belongs to me, from eight to five, and it's not time for her to clock out – not yet.

I had lived that type of lifestyle once before. I had fought most of my teenage life, but I changed my life for the best. Thomas left the building, and then Katherine began yelling at me. She was upset that I destroyed a relationship that didn't even exist.

I said to her, there is no relationship. She asked me, "How would you know about real love? I haven't seen one woman come through this door."

Little did she know that my true love was standing here arguing with me. I pulled her toward me, and I kissed her again. Then I swept my hand across her face and rubbed my finger against her lips.

I told her; I have loved you since the first day I saw you. I wanted to marry you! I cheated; I made plenty of mistakes. I was trying to offer you the material things in life, but all you asked for was my time. Now I am ready to give you that, but you must let go of this unhealthy relationship.

I kissed her again and then repeated it again and again, I love you! I was trying to beat it inside of her head, without my hands but with my words. Katherine rushed home and left me standing there.

I called Katherine's phone to check up on her, but she didn't answer. I kept calling and calling and driving around in circles. I wanted to rush to her house, but I didn't want her to be upset with me.

Katherine finally answered. I ask her where she was? She immediately started telling me about all her problems indirectly. I stopped the car and sat at the green light. It took a few seconds to take it all in.

When she confessed to me that she wanted to commit suicide; I had to calm myself. I rubbed my head. I told her I couldn't let that happen! The day that Katherine dies my spirit dies — I will die.

I felt it again, Ba-Bum. I can't leave her alone. She told me that she was at the Seashore Beach.

I begged her to wait for me. I drove as fast as I could to get to her and prayed, I didn't get stopped. When I arrived, she was sitting near the water.

I ran to her— she was dripping wet, bloody, and severely beaten. I covered my face in grief, and I walked off for a second; it was bothersome.

I was angry at Thomas, but I was also mad at Katherine. I felt a rage of violence overcoming me before I ever allowed Thomas to hit Katherine again, or see her shed another tear. I promised to do whatsoever it took to save her, even if it meant going back to prison.

I apologized because I didn't keep her safe. I took off my shirt and asked her to take off her wet clothes.

Then I asked her to stay with me until she healed, and we figured this out. When I got home, I quickly picked up the phone to call the police, but Katherine hung it up.

I sighed in frustration, but I respected her decision. I called her parents to tell them that she was okay. I invited them over and gave them the address.

They were confused, but they immediately came over!

Mr. Roosevelt asked, "Why is Katherine with you? Are you and Katherine in a relationship? More to the point, exactly who are you to Katherine at this point?"

Mr. Roosevelt didn't know anything about me.

Then I saw Mrs. Roosevelt; she asked, "Are you, Jason, — the Jason that dated Katherine in high school."

Yes, I am.

"Where is she?"

She's in my bedroom.

"Your bedroom?" said Mr. Roosevelt as his eyes widened.

Let me take you to her. Then I walked away.

Mr. Roosevelt turned to his wife. "Why is Katherine in his bedroom?"

"Shhh!' Mrs. Roosevelt said.

I suppose they had forgotten I was standing there, or they didn't care. I went into the bathroom and lit several candles, filled the bathtub with warm water, and turned off the lights. I gave Katherine's and her parents a little privacy.

After they left, I carried Katherine into the bathroom and then walked away. Katherine said, "Don't go; can you please help me get undressed."

I walked up to her and then took off the shirt that I had given her. She was naked; the first thing I noticed was her chest and firm nipples.

Katherine was slightly embarrassed. She dropped her head; then I lifted it. I held her by the arm as she stepped into the warm water. I began bathing her with a sponge.

Although she was swollen and bruised; I thought she was the most beautiful woman in the world. She seduced me with her beauty.

But I knew she was vulnerable, and I didn't want to take advantage of her in such a weak state. Katherine desired to touch me, and she did right between the thighs. Although I wished to have her, I grabbed her by the hand to stop her.

I wanted to wait until she healed entirely. She told me,

"Please, just hold me."

I couldn't deny those big brown puppy eyes. I took off my clothes, but I left on my undergarments and then I joined Katherine in the bathtub.

I wrapped my arms and legs around her tightly and pacified her pain until she fell asleep in my arms. Then I carried her to my bed and lay her down; she fell back to sleep.

When I pulled the blanket up; I noticed several soft cuts across her inner wrist. The scars were small; I couldn't tell if they were old scratches or fresh cut marks.

I rubbed my finger across her wrist; Katherine woke up, turned over, and then she started to cry. Her tears were unbearable, but they confirmed my belief.

I wanted to take away her pain without stripping her self-respect. I lay beside Katherine and held her all night.

Katherine –

The next morning, I smelled breakfast cooking. I held my head up; I saw Jason sitting on the edge of the bed, watching me as I slept.

I tried to move, but I was in too much pain. Jason told me to stay in bed; he went to the kitchen and came back with a breakfast bed tray filled with treats.

Jason invited me to stay with him at his beach house; it was out of the country. He wanted to take care of me until I completely healed, but I was afraid of the after-effects. Thomas would kill me.

"You're already dead!" said Jason. "You're living the life that he desires for you; there is no freedom to think for yourself. You can't make any decision on your own. That's not your life or your dream; it's his."

Why do you care so much? I asked. No one else ever did. No men have ever rescued me. Furthermore, a Knight in Shining Armor – it doesn't exist; I have been waiting for him for months, and he never showed up.

Jason shook his head sadly. "You have to be fair; you never mentioned anything to anyone, so how could they help you?"

He kissed me. I never said I was a knight, you did, but I do promise to protect you." He smiled.

"Your knight has arrived, and I guarantee you the life that you have been searching for, the life no one ever promised you, can start today."

I knew Jason was the man of my dreams. That fairytale story that I had heard about and dreamed of did exist, love existed. I felt it, saw it, and was living it for the first time. I was in love!

Jason asked, "Will you come with me to the beach house?"

I nodded. Yes, I will stay, but only until I heal.

"I'm relieved!" said Jason, and then he called his secretary. He turned on the speaker phone.

"Northeastern Oil and Gas Corporation, this is Elizabeth, how can I help you?"

Elizabeth, Katherine, and I will be off until further notice.

"Thomas has come to the office several times looking for Katherine."

Jason said, "She's safe with me. Do not give Thomas any information at all.

Then I told my parents that I was going out of town with Jason. We were going to his beach house in the tropical islands. Mum questioned me, "Are you sure that's a wise decision?"

We arrived just before nightfall on his private jet.

First, he showered, and then he disappeared. The long flight drained me; so, I spoiled myself with a long bath. After I finished, I covered my body with lavender bath oils and perfumes.

I slid into a floor-length silk gown with a high slit and a low-cut, which revealed my perfect cleavage. I sat in a tall chair next to the fireplace to catch my breath; I had never seen such a fantastic sight.

Glass windows were everywhere. It was white sand and light turquoise water, the beach house rested high on a dune, next to the seashore.

The sun was starting to set; the beautiful sky was orange,

with a grayish color, and the moon peeked just above the ocean waters.

The wind was blowing slowly, and the waves were beating against the sand. When it became darker, the stars lit up the sky.

He had dinner, dessert, and glasses of wine placed on the table. Candles lit; the scenery was romantic as hell, and we were in a lustful mood.

Jason sat behind me and wrapped his arms around my neck. He asked the servers to leave. I turned my head toward him and let him gently kiss my lips.

He slid his tongue inside my mouth, and we began kissing passionately, mouth to mouth. We were hungry, but it wasn't the meal that we were interested in eating.

Jason pulled away; he pulled the freshly cooked, garlic, buttery lobster out of the shell. He fed me bite-size pieces.

I wanted to have more than the lobster. Jason's chest was my main course, and it was more tempting than dinner. I turned completely around.

He slid his hand inside of my gown; he rubbed and squeezed my leg as he fed me from his lips. I wanted to say "Stop," but my feelings were too powerful, they overcame me, and I submitted to his gentle touch!

I stopped eating and then turned my body around; I wrapped my legs around Jason's waist but, still clothed, I sat on top of him.

I smiled – because I knew what I was doing to his mind; he was enticed, and I had him right where I wanted him. I tried to stand up, but he pulled me back down.

That's just what I predicted, he desired me, and I needed him. We began kissing intensely.

It was windy, and dinner waited. We were exploding with passion. Jason stood up with my legs, still wrapped around his waist. He pushed the plates aside and laid me on the table. But I wasn't ready to take such a significant step, not yet.

"Wait!" I said. But I already knew he was going to be the one that I marry. I just wanted our honeymoon to be unique. Jason gazed at me with a deep passion in his eyes.

Then he stroked my upper thigh with his hand; he gripped it tightly. He rubbed his finger down the middle of my face and then leaned down and kissed me.

"Whoa!" he looked into my eyes and said, "Stop teasing me!"

Why not, when I enjoy it? I replied.

Jason –

Armed with time, I had the exact tool that I needed to steal Katherine's entrapped heart. I invited her to stay with me until she healed completely.

I was going to bandage Katherine's wounds, both inside and out. I planned to sweep her off her feet, and then make her my wife.

However, I needed some time, and I was going to take advantage of the clock, – time. Katherine could not heal in one night. Her life was difficult.

When we arrived in the islands, I took a shower and then rushed to complete Katherine's surprise dinner. I hired a catering service. They were on the patio, preparing and setting up everything for our arrival.

After I showered, I went outside while Katherine bathed. I needed to see how things were going. Then Katherine walked into the kitchen, with a white gown on.

It was a bigger tease than she ever imagined. Katherine looked ravishing, and she smelled like roses. I was fighting back a desire to take Katherine straight to my bedroom.

I wanted to lay her down and rest on top of her if you get my drift. But, much as I wanted her, I didn't want to be with her under these conditions. I desired to make love to her for the first time as my wife.

I walked up to her with a blindfold in my hand. I covered Katherine's eyes and whispered in her ear I have a surprise for you. I kissed her on the neck and escorted her onto the patio. I had hired the best catering service in the country to prepare dinner.

When I had her in place, I removed the blindfold. I thanked the servers and asked them to leave. Katherine and we began eating our meal and kissing.

I tried to pull her gown straps down, but Katherine kept pushing them back up. I laid my head against her firm chest and I caressed her back and hugged her tightly. I may have touched a few body parts that I shouldn't have, but she kept stopping me.

My passion for her was hard to control, and I needed a fire extinguisher to put out the blaze that was inside my pants. She knew what to do to arouse me. I desired to wait; however, it was becoming harder to do.

I rubbed my hand over my head and yelled out. My sexual frustration was agonizing me. I hit the table with my fist. I took long and deep breaths trying to calm down.

I kissed Katherine on the lips. She apologized, but Katherine wasn't sorry. She enjoyed teasing me.

Excuse me; I said as I walked away from the dinner table; I went into the bathroom and took another shower. Katherine stayed behind and cleaned up everything before she went to bed.

After she finished, she went into the guest room to sleep. But she couldn't, nor could I. I got up and knocked on the bedroom door; she asked me to come in, and I did.

I pulled the cover back and joined her on the bed. I wrapped my leg around her leg, I cradled her tightly, and we fell asleep.

CHAPTER 13

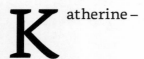**K** atherine –

The next morning, Jason and I got dressed. We went out to eat breakfast. Although I had my own money, I enjoyed letting Jason spoil me as if I was his queen. Besides, according to him, he adored making me smile.

Every devoted moment we fell more and more in love with each other, and we completed one another. Jason continued to surprise me with gifts; he showered me with affection. Then he took me to his yacht.

Does everything that belongs to you look so gorgeous?

Jason hesitated and then said, "Everything – every single thing in my life but you, because you don't belong to me, not yet."

Jason sat on the couch, and I sat on his lap. We kissed, but Jason wasn't falling for that leg-puller again. He spun me around until I was lying on my back. Then he got up to fix us a drink.

Jason asked, "What happened?"

What happened?

"Yes, with you and Thomas."

I took a deep breath. Well — we were all hanging out with someone named Mindy. We were at her house. I don't know how we ended up there.

I guess I was a friend of a friend; Sandy asked me to come. We were out having a little fun. Thomas walked up to us and introduced himself.

He seemed to care for me. I told Thomas what University I was attending; he said to me, "I'm going there as well.

It was strange because I never saw him on the campus. We started dating, but whatever. I questioned him several times about going to the same school, and he told me that he lived with a friend off-campus.

I can't recall seeing him. That night he became protective of me. I thought it was weird, but adorable how he shadowed me; he must've been attracted to me, right?

I grimaced. Yes, it was a little too soon, but some people fall in love on the first date, although it wasn't a date and I wasn't in love.

Jason smirked. "A few minutes and you thought he was in love."

I thought I had that type of effect on men. Wouldn't you agree?

"I plead the fifth."

I continued. Anyways, I sat with my friends and some other students that I knew. Katie and Maryann didn't like him, but that wasn't their decision.

Thomas sat with the group; he sat next to Christopher Wilbur. Christopher was dating Sandy; we were drinking and enjoying one another's company. Christopher danced away with Sandy.

I paused, and Jason said, "Continue…"

Well — we left early; Thomas walked us to the car and kissed me on the cheek goodnight. He said he would see me around.

My friends and I went home. From that day on, we kept meeting each other somewhere on campus. The hallways, outside of the cafeteria, I believe Thomas was searching for me; again, I have that type of effect on men.

I looked at Jason with a playful smile. But that's enough about us.

"There is more to the story, I'm sure."

Yes, Thomas began hitting me; that's the end of the story.

"You have a lot of endings."

Katherine didn't want to continue talking; there were too many bad memories. A tear dropped, and Jason wiped it away.

Jason raised his voice, "That is what I will not tolerate! I'll take care of that. But, don't you – don't you dare cry. That will never happen again. Now, come here."

Katherine nodded. "Yes, I can recall the day I called in to request a month off due to a family emergency, well, I was involved in a crisis.

I think it was our second or third fight. I was in the kitchen arguing about something; I don't remember. Then Thomas started beating me in the stomach.

I was in so much pain; I just wanted it to stop. I reached for the pot of hot water that was boiling on the stove and threw it at him.

It splashed on his arm. He screamed in pain, but he let go of me. I ran and locked myself inside the bedroom, hoping after the pain was gone that he would calm down.

But, instead, he kicked the door down, and then began beating me and beating me. He didn't break my bones, but it felt like it.

"I am sorry!" Jason said.

Don't be.

"What happened next?"

The same thing repeatedly, "I remember when we went to the store one day; he was parked in front of the entrance door, sitting in the car on the driver's side. A man who Thomas nor I had never seen before until that day opened the door for me. Why would he do that?

When I got into the car, Thomas grabbed my neck and choked me. He squeezed it tighter and tighter until I couldn't breathe. I couldn't even cough!

I started hitting the seat because I was too afraid to fight back.

Then Thomas let go and told me if I thought about being with another man, the next time he wouldn't let go.

I sat there as tear after tear fell, but I never said a word. That was just one of the horror stories. There were times that he hit me just because he assumed, I was cheating.

No man would open a door for a woman unless he knows her, right? The best part is that everyone looked, but no one stopped to help.

Then there was this time when he wanted to have sex with me, and I refused. This one is hysterical; I promise! He grabbed the pillow from the bed, I – thinking back.

I don't know why I wasn't expecting a foolish reaction, but I was surprised. Thomas put...umm, the pillow over my head and pressed it down as hard as he could, which was not unusual at this point.

I started kicking because I couldn't breathe. What was even more hysterical is that I wanted to stop breathing. Finally, I pretended to pass out; I stopped moving. Thomas removed the pillow from my head.

I heard him say I should have taken it. I kept my eyes closed, but I was praying, please don't. He kicked me between my legs with the back of his heel; the pain was unendurable, but I was afraid to grunt.

He beat me many times, but I have become much stronger. I was praying that he would walk away, and he did.

Then the night of the Christmas party. I was overwhelmed by tears.

That animal said, are you hot for him? He must have known I was. Maybe he smelled my passion for you?

I was saving myself for you, but that didn't quite work out. More tears fell down my cheek. "I inhaled the scent of Thomas' strong cologne...well, enough of Thomas and me.

"What happened?"

Do you have to ask?

"He raped you?"

I turned my head away. Jason wrapped his arms around me; we cuddled and watched lots of love movies.

Jason –

But I couldn't stop thinking about what Katherine had said. Her distress became my distress. Katherine must have known I was enraged; she began throwing pillows at me to lighten my mood.

I started tickling her. She pulled my arm and said, "Let's dance," I kissed her.

Katherine –

I was happier than ever; my heart was utterly smiling!

Jason asked, "When did you know?"

Know what?

"That you loved me!"

I laughed as I looked at him. At first, I didn't know that I cared as much as I did, but I knew you was in love with me, and that pulled me in even more.

"How?"

How, because there were over fifty people at the recital, but the only sincere smile was yours. The way you looked at me – I never saw anyone look at me like that before.

"I was looking at someone else."

I hit him with the pillow, and then we laughed and kissed. I didn't want to think about Thomas or our problems; I left all that baggage in Washington, D.C.

Jason was tired; he fell asleep with his head on my lap, and his arm wrapped around my waist. I moved Jason's arm and lifted his head and laid it on the couch.

I began writing, which was one of my hobbies. I was trying to describe in words how I felt for Jason. I had gone through at least ten sheets of paper trying to find the perfect words.

I tossed poem after poem into the trash can. There were no perfect words. How could I describe something that I couldn't explain? How could I describe it accurately?

I knew it sounded crazy, but it was the truth. I had never been in love before. Yes, I was expecting to feel some tenderness for Jason, but this was more. Katherine balled up the poems and threw them away. I went on the deck, lay down on the lounge chair, and dozed off.

Jason –

I eventually woke up and noticed Katherine gone. I was going to find her when I spotted a piece of paper balled-up on the floor. Katherine must've missed the garbage can.

Should I read it, I contemplated. No, I thought to myself, and I threw the paper back inside the trash can and walked away, but I was curious. I walked back to the garbage can and saw several other sheets of paper. But I grabbed the one from the top and read it,

> The agonizing pain that I have endured
> Day after day the same thing;
> Disfigured inside and out.
> I could not escape, although
> I gave it all my might
> Over and over, I lost the fight
> Where is my knight?

I am here, I whispered. After I read the first few lines of the poem, I can hear Katherine's voice crying out for help. But I couldn't help her. I continued reading,

> A tear drops down my face;
> Because I have made the biggest mistake of my life
> Trying to find love in the wrong place
> Instead, I got beaten
> My heart has become colder than winter snow
> Scars tattooed on my wrist;
> In the color of a rust-colored brittle crayon.
> I'm crying out loud
> But no one hears me since there is no sound;

Katherine woke up; she saw tears flowing from my eyes. I stopped reading. She asked me to continue. We sat down. This

Shelley Jenkins

time she sat behind me and wrapped her legs around my waist as
she read the rest,

He tore my heart apart; I needed a surgeon
I'm stressing over these heavy burdens;
God help me
Before my soul descends to the grave,
deliver me
Send me the perfect gentlemen that will say
I am here to save thee.
Let my hero come through the front door
And tell me, Katherine,
You don't have to cry anymore.
Then I heard a knock:
One...two...three...four
I opened the door. Hello!
"My name is Jason,"
Did you come to save me?
What brought you this way, Jason?
"I heard your heart crying so,
The wind dragged me in."
Well, come in
Pl-please break these shackles,
break these chains
That restrains me,
Free me, so, I could love again.
You have the key to the lock
and the entrance...
Your stay – is endless; limitless
Without you, I would be eternally restless
Rescue me from his jealousy, before
he sends me to the cemetery
Love me senseless,
let it weaken me,
Kiss me until I'm breathless
Make my heart skip a beat

Touch me and leave me helpless,
make me defenseless
I am strength-less,
but you came and defended me
Jason,
Thank you,
For removing the handcuffs
Thank you,
For telling Thomas,
that's enough
Thank you,
For reconstructing me
and renewing my trust again
Thank you,
You gave me back my confidence
and not honoring my death wish
Thank you,
For loving me for an eternity

I turned around and kissed Katherine, and we wiped away each other's tears. I felt the sincerity of her broken heart. I wanted to soothe her pain for the rest of my life, and Katherine attempted to love me for the rest of hers'.

Thomas –

I reached out to everyone attempting to find Katherine, but I couldn't locate her. She was well hidden. I called Katherine's cell phone several times, and I left threatening messages, I begged her to come home. However, Katherine's cell phone was turned off.

I assured Katherine that I would find her, and when I do, it would be her last day alive. I couldn't think without Katherine. I started drinking alcohol heavily. My boss and co-workers became concerned.

I began messing up clients' case files. We appeared at the hearings, but the wrong case information was in the folders. Due to my mistake's cases were dropped. The law firm recommended that I stay home and get myself together and clear my mind. But nothing could heal my broken heart. I needed Katherine.

Also, I had a secret; her name is Mindy Black. I loved Katherine wholeheartedly, and she meant everything to me. So, I was willing to take down anyone who stood between us.

Mindy and I had a relationship that had been on and off since high school. I lived with Mindy for years. She was just a fling; I told my friends.

Furthermore, she was more than that; she was my child's mother, and Katherine was clueless about our relationship and my child. Mindy's best friend, Sandy, was also Katherine's friend.

When I was on campus, I had to be very careful; I couldn't get caught. Now, are things starting to make sense? I had to have control over Katherine, so, I could always keep an eye on her. That way, I could do all the things I desired, and she would be too afraid to leave.

I loved manipulating her. Besides, what would Katherine say if she saw me with Mindy and the baby? She would end the relationship.

I knew Mindy wasn't going anywhere. There had been many other women, yet she stood right there beside me. Mindy loved me, and I enjoyed Katherine.

While Katherine was away, I took my son to my parents' house and invited Mindy over to Katherine's house, and she came. Maybe she could replace Katherine, I thought.

Mindy suspected that I was seeing someone else, but she had never seen her before, so she thought. Portraits of Katherine with friends and family were hanging throughout the house. Her awards and degrees hung on the wall as well.

Mindy asked, "Does she work with you? I saw you talking to her at the party. She's beautiful and sophisticated, the opposite of me."

Mindy looked around and wished she had it all: her looks, money, education, and me. She needed just a little bit of this woman's strength. I said, "Mindy – I love you just the way you are; you don't have to become Katherine. However, for a moment, I desired Mindy to be Katherine.

"Yes, I do…I have a son, and I have nothing to offer him other than love. You refuse to marry me because you're not ready to settle down and I'm accepting it because I'm in love with you, so being Mindy is not enough."

I sighed. You are my first love and my child's mother; no one could compare to that. While Katherine was away, we were eating dinner, bathing, and drinking glasses of wine in the tub.

We were having sex in Katherine's bed; Mindy was enjoying the exquisite lifestyle.

However, I was not satisfied with just having sex with Mindy. I enjoyed having the cake and the pie, but the one wasn't as good without the other.

The thought of Katherine having sex with another man was excruciating. I was going insane; I needed her to help me cope with my anger, my desires, and to ease my obsession.

I had never shown that type of aggression toward Mindy before. Katherine was the only person who had dealt with those demons, and she kept it to herself.

Mindy said, "I am not trying to replace Katherine, and I'm not going anywhere. Although I wasn't faithful, I was a dependable father.

CHAPTER 14

J ason –

I was upset; I wished Katherine would have expressed her most deep-felt feelings much sooner since I felt the same way about her.

I loved her as much or more from the first day I saw her reciting her first poem out loud.

But Katherine wasn't ready for a relationship then. No matter how frustrated I wanted to be, I couldn't stay mad for long.

Especially when I looked into Katherine's beautiful big eyes, it was hard for me to keep my cool when I stood next to her – I felt things rising which could only be shot down by her.

We walked on the dock, and I stood behind her. I was at my peak. I lifted Katherine's shirt and unsnapped her bra.

I placed my hand inside her blouse and massaged her breast. Katherine's neck fell back against my chest; I kissed her neckline as she moaned my name.

I massaged her heart with soft caresses, and then slightly turn her head towards my face. She parted her lips; I grazed my tongue slowly across the edge of them. I began kissing her gently as I slid my tongue inside her mouth, circling my tongue around hers, caressing her tongue gracefully.

Her kisses were sweet and luscious. Katherine's heart was melting with each second. Her nipples were expanding, by the touch of my warm hands and tender touch.

Katherine closed her eyes as my hands cuff her breast. I kindly slide my fingers down her pants and play with her clit. She grabs my wrist to guide me to that perfect spot. I rub gentle yet firm until she wets my fingers with her juices.

Katherine moans, her voice starts to crack as she starts to climax. I stop and shamefully taste my finger.

I asked the driver to take us home before things got out of control. But Katherine wasn't ready to leave.

Therefore, I held her, still kissing her as we watched the moon reflect on the beach. It was windy; she felt a chill and quivered. I wrapped my arms around her and kissed her on the neck.

Katherine decides to please me as well. She slides her hands down my pants, and she begins stroking my penis.

However, I grabbed her wrist to stop her; I knew if she awakened the penis, there was no stopping me.

Then I grabbed Katherine's hand and ran to the bar. I grabbed a bottle of wine, and we hurried to the hot tub. I sat at one end of the spa, and Katherine sat at the other. She removed her bra; she had on nothing but, red lace panties. I began massaging her feet and kissing them.

I pulled her by the legs toward me; she was sitting on my thighs, grinding me, moving her hips and butt up and down in circular motion. I stare at her as I began sucking her nipples intensely.

I began pulling her panties down. I stop myself and rest my head between her breasts.

We were drinking and talking until we reached the beach house. When we got there, we went to bed. I whispered in her ear, each night when I lie next to you, I get closer and closer to you.

She said, "Each night that I spend with you, my heart gets farther and farther apart from Thomas. I love you!"

Katherine lay in my arms as I held her tightly. I didn't want to turn her loose. "Although I wanted to escape Thomas, I wanted you to capture me," said Katherine. "I feel strong again and confident in who I am," she said.

Katherine –

I was having a great time. Nothing mattered to me. Especially my cell phone, I never turned it on, or listened to any of Thomas' messages.

Although, I didn't answer the phone; the calls never stopped. I had over thirty messages on my phone, and all of them were from Thomas.

They were hostile words; he was threatening my life. I replayed the recordings to Jason.

Jason said, "I assure you that it is nothing for you to be concerned over. I will protect you, and I promise you that."

I am ready to talk to him; I want to tell him that I have made my decision.

"What is your decision?"

I smiled. Wouldn't you like to know?

Jason chuckled "I already know, I can see it in your eyes, and they don't lie. Are you sure you're ready for me?"

Yes, and are you sure you are ready for me?

"Yes!" He started tickling me; he enjoyed seeing me laugh and smile. Then he stopped.

Jason is this how it feels to be in love? She knew Jason was the one for her.

"How does it feel?"

Amazing!

Jason kissed me. He said, "If you need me to intervene or mediate, just hand me the phone."

I think I can handle this, I said

He held me in his arms; I called my parents first to let them know how I was doing. I asked my father if he could go to my house to make sure everything was okay. I also wanted to make sure Thomas was there when I called. My father said, "okay."

Thomas –

I heard a car pull up; Mr. and Mrs. Roosevelt must have seen my car parked in the driveway. The doorbell rang.

But I was already putting on my pajama pants and a robe. Be calm, and Run, I told Mindy. She rushed into Katherine's bedroom. I answered the door to Katherine's parents.

I stood outside, and I started closing the door behind me. Katherine's mother placed her hand on the door and pushed it open.

Mrs. Roosevelt said, "Could we come in?"

I hesitated but finally said, yes.

"Why did you hesitate?"

I have a woman inside, I said. They didn't think the joke was humorous at all. I asked them, so what brought you over? Have you heard from Katherine?

Mr. Roosevelt said, "We came to see what is going on and to find out where is our daughter."

Katherine hasn't returned home, and I am worried sick about her.

Mrs. Roosevelt said, "I know the truth."

Do you? What is the truth?

"My daughter is in danger; I can feel it."

And you haven't called the police – what type of parents are you? Or has Katherine called you? They could not lie, but Thomas knew the truth.

"Where is my daughter?" She clapped her hands together; she acted if she wanted to strike me just like I hit her daughter.

Is there a problem?

"Yes, there is. Where IS my daughter? Thomas, I am tired of playing this stupid game with you."

I said your daughter left me, and I have no clue where she went, but when you do hear from her, please tell her that I am going insane without her, I stare vacantly.

"It's strange how she left and didn't contact you. Can you explain what happened again? Do we need to call the police; I am extremely concerned about my daughter."

So, am I, but she will call; this has happened before? But she never stayed away for this long.

Mrs. Roosevelt gave me a suspicious glance. "Happened before? I am confused; how often does this happen?"

I stopped talking when my phone rang; it was Mindy calling me from the bedroom. It was great timing. "Get rid of them, this bed is getting cold and so am I. Come back to bed.

I pretended to be on a business call with the firm. I'll be there, I said. Turning to the parents, I said, I must get ready for work, which was a lie because I was given time off.

Finally, Katherine's idiotic parents left. I went back to the bedroom and lay on top of Mindy. Then the phone rang. I answered it, and it was Katherine. I jumped up and began yelling at her.

I shouted, "Where are you? You haven't been to work, nor have you been answering your phone. The office told me that Jason hadn't returned either.

What's going on, talk to me. Are you with your boss? It doesn't matter; I forgive you. Just come home." I swayed nervously at the edge of the bed.

What words might woo the harlot back to me? "I miss you, and I love you!" I was looking at Mindy the whole time. Then I repeated, "I care for you."

I was contemplating – how badly I wanted to beat Katherine senseless for leaving the house and me. But I was happy to hear from her.

"I don't care about your heartaches or love," she said.

Oh, you will, and I am not leaving this house, so you will have to face me.

I heard that idiot in the background, Jason asks her to give him the phone. She put her hand over it. I listened to her muffled words, "No, I don't want things to get out of hand; if Thomas heard your voice, he would kill me, Katherine mumbled." They were already on my death list.

Jason said, "It's already out of hand." Finally, I interrupted, "Jason is talking in the background, huh; well tell him that I have a magazine waiting for him and a forty caliber." She said, "Leave my house and take your few belongings with you."

"I am asking you nicely as possible; and like you always say, 'We can do this the easy or the hard way. It doesn't matter to me. Thomas, I'm more than willing to do it the hard way'. I am tired of being beaten, and the rape is unpardonable."

"So, keep your apologies; I don't want them. They cannot take away my pain or give me back my virginity or the time I wasted caring for you."

I couldn't reply. Mindy was sitting next to me. Mindy had never seen that side of me, angry and cursing.

Katherine said, "Do you understand that I have been miserable for the last few months? I don't deserve this. I want to be free."

Freedom always comes at a price, Katherine. The question is, what price you are willing to pay for it? I am not going anywhere. So, when you return home, I'll still be here waiting for you.

"I can't take this anymore."

Yes, you are going to take this and more.

"What does that mean?"

Are you hanging with Jason? If so, tell him my issue is no longer with you, but with him as well. He wanted you — well, we are a full package, and I'm willing to fight for you.

"Yes, I am with Jason, and I love him!"

Do you like that oil and gas grease parrot?

"No, I love him!"

Do you love him? I began to lose control; I begged her to come home. But she refused.

Have you been with him sexually? I asked.

"That isn't any of your business; the relationship is over."

Katherine, the next time your parents see you it will be in a body bag or a casket. Are you willing to pay that price? Are you ready to die for Jason? Or is he prepared to die for you?

"We are willing to die for each other."

I said; Let me ask the punk a question?

Jason grabbed the phone and said, "I'm right here."

I, she, or you will die before I give her to you!

During our conversation, Mindy started feeling nauseous; she hopped up from the bed and ran to the bathroom. I angrily hung up the phone and followed her. She moaned, "I had too many glasses of wine."

Are you okay?

"I guess I'm just a little tipsy from the wine. Let's go back to bed." When Mindy woke up the next morning, she was sick again.

She told me, "I'm not feeling well; she'd better not be pregnant. That made me mad, but I said, "Maybe you're hungry, let's go and get breakfast."

She nodded half-willingly. Mindy and I were getting dressed to go out of town to eat breakfast; I didn't want anyone to spot us together.

Mindy –

I was packing my belongings, and I took them with me. On the way to the restaurant, I asked Thomas to stop by the store so I could grab a drink.

I went inside and bought a pregnancy test and a bottle of water. After I paid for it, I stuffed the pregnancy test inside of my purse and walked back to the car.

When I arrived home, I rushed into the bathroom and immediately took the test; it was the most intense three minutes of my life. The stopwatch beeped.

I looked at the result; it was positive. I was excited, but I was afraid to tell Thomas. I tore the bag and wrapped a piece of it around the test and stuffed it back inside my purse.

I would have to wait for the right time to show Thomas the results.

CHAPTER 15

On the other side of the country far away, Jason was showering Katherine with love. She was waking up to dozens of red roses and breakfast in bed as a symbol of his love.

They were spending their last day out of the country. Jason was wondering how he could make the day unforgettable.

He decided to take her on a date–just the two of them. But how could he make it unique? He rented a small room just for them.

He told Katherine that they were going to pick up something to wear and then go out to eat. He asked her to choose the color of their outfits, and she decided on silver.

He hired the best catering services and decorators; he ordered her favorite wine and flowers. Flowers were all over the building.

Pink rose petals spread across the floor. Red was Katherine's favorite color, but he chose pink for the occasion.

They went shopping together, but when they went into the store, they separated. Katherine bought a pair of diamond earrings, a long silver satin gown, and she added heels and her favorite perfume.

After they returned to the beach house, he showered and left. He told Katherine that the chauffeur would pick her up. Jason wanted to combine memories from the prom and the Christmas party and mix them with new ones.

He started getting dressed at the building. He put on a silver satin suit, white shirt, gray dress shoes, and a gray, pink and white striped tie.

Katherine arrived later; the building was elegant. Jason looked handsome, and she was gorgeous. The back of the dress was draped with a scoop down to the lower part of her back, and the front had a smaller drape scoop between her breasts. He told her she was beautiful!

Since roses were Katherine's favorite flower, pink roses were everywhere, and a card was sitting on the table.

The lights were dim. Jason played the exact song that was playing when they first met, "Forever" by Kenny G.

She looked into Jason's eyes. They told the original story; he was in love with her.

Katherine wondered, "How could someone fall in love over and over again?" She closed her eyes; she felt weak in the heart.

Love was starting to take over her mind. "That's how I want you to feel every day, helplessly in love all over and over, and over again."

He took her to the table and then handed her the card; it expressed his feelings perfectly. The music was still playing.

The card said,
Out of all the women that I've ever met,
And I've encountered plenty
Something was special about our first date
The touch of your warm, tender hands
Sped up my heart rate; palpitations – fluttering
Pound, pounding against my chest
It was out of control our love
I danced around the dance floor with you in my arms
My beautiful lady
I lifted you in the air as if you were flying leaping from cloud to cloud
I was dreaming
Could this be the winning ticket?
Standing in front of me

Swinging those erotic hips
Biting those sexy lips
My heart had pre-selected you
No other woman could rock as hard as you
It was a few rivalries, but no one could fill your shoes
No other woman could target my heart
I heard a voice; it said to me
She's the woman
Look into them dreamy diamond brown eyes
And that graceful smile
She will help you conquer the world
And she will be right there by your side
There's no need to postpone the wedding any longer
Let your hearts beat
Bond and become one;
It seems like fate put you directly into my path
and destiny won
And I have been celebrating that day ever since
Our love is complicated—
But it's incredible
When I stare into your eyes, I'm paralyzed.
When you say, "I love you!" I am fascinated;
I feel butterflies you say likewise
Well, bring me those lovely thick thighs
and that fresh hot apple pie
I want to pound, pound between your thighs
Kiss you passionately
On those sugary lips
Wrap your legs around my thighs tightly
Let my love carry you high above the clouds
Until I hear you yell – scream Oh, Oh my!"
Baby, no one or anything could be as sweet as this pie
Cut straight from the middle of your thigh
The only thing that could make me moan so loud,
"Oh dear, Oh my, my, my!

They finished eating dinner, and then they danced until midnight. At precisely midnight dozens, and dozens of pink rose petals fell from the ceiling. Katherine started smiling and crying simultaneously!

She wasn't ready to leave, and she wasn't prepared to face reality, it was time to meet with Thomas. She spent the best two weeks of her life with Jason.

They went back to the beach house, and then they went to bed. Katherine held onto Jason tightly, and he did the same.

Jason smiled and asked, "Where do we go from here?"

Katherine said, "I don't know."

Jason said, "Come to live at my place, Katherine, I can't let you go; I crave to spend my life with you. Furthermore, I cannot let him harm you again."

Katherine knew she would be safe there. But would Thomas leave them alone? The Thomas she knew may be willing to murder them. She couldn't allow Jason to lose his life because of her.

Katherine –

We were packing our bags. I was stuffing the last bag, and I broke down in tears, I was afraid. I had mixed feelings about leaving.

Jason asked, "Are you okay, or do we need to stay a few more days or weeks?"

I attempted a smile. No, I think I'm ready.

"Ready for what…to be with him or me?"

You!

We kissed and finished packing. Then we headed to the jet. I was ready to turn the page and begin a new chapter.

While we were on the plane, we talked about the moments we spent together. I cherished every second that I spent with Jason.

We arrived in Washington D. C. I was so tired that I decided to spend the night with Jason. I called my parents, sisters, and friends to let them know that I was in town.

The bruises had healed, but some marks were still visible. Jason had suffocated me with so much love; the injuries that were on my face, I didn't even notice anymore. Jason healed the pain that was in my heart.

Maryann, Katie, Brittany, and Samantha came straight over; they wanted to hear about my trip. I put on a robe and sat on the balcony and waited for them to arrive. I felt like a teenager who was in love for the first time.

When everyone arrived, Jason walked them to the terrace, and then he served us drinks and snacks. They thanked him for his generosity and for taking such good care of me.

He said, "It was my pleasure!" As soon as he walked away, they began asking me what happened. First, I apologized for keeping my life a secret.

The truth is I let out a slow sigh. Thomas has been beating me for months. Samantha said, "Why would you keep that type of secret to yourself?"

I was afraid and ashamed. Thomas had stolen my virginity. I attempted to kill myself numerous of times, but something always stopped me.

They began to mourn for me. But I was too strong to allow my family and friends to feel pity for me.

Don't you dare feel sympathy or cry for me, I said.

I held my head down for a moment. I remembered Jason saying, "Only God can look down on me."

I lifted my head. Jason rescued me from depression, abuse, fear, and loneliness. I was in love with him since the prom; however, Marcy got pregnant, and we separated. We had so much respect for one another from day one, but things had gotten much stronger at the Employee's Christmas Party.

Then I told them about the dream-like trip we had just taken. Jason had taken great care of me, and I enjoyed every minute of being pampered. Seeing how much he loved me. It was extraordinary.

We kissed each other goodnight, and they left, so, I could get some rest. But I didn't want to sleep.

Jason and I played and wrestled. Jason knew all that physical activity would spark sexual responses. So, he didn't want to roll around with me too much.

Besides, if that made me happy, it made him happy. After we finished playing, we wrapped our arms around each other and kissed.

I said, "Since you have been in my life, my heart has created a new melody. It's like a piano when the musician plays every note correctly.

I don't know if you hear the same music when I hold you."

Jason said, "Oh, I see stars within my reach, things that I thought were impossible are becoming imaginable. I don't hear music, but I understand your cries. I feel your pain. I see your fear, and I taste your love."

"We have a bond that no one could ever break, not even Thomas. Although we don't have any legal documents that say that you're Ms. Taylor, you will always be that."

He pointed at my chest. "You have never said it, but I know your heart belongs to me." I nodded with a huge smile. "It does."

CHAPTER 16

K atherine knew it was that time; she had to face Thomas. Oh, how she dreaded that moment. Three days after she returned to Washington, D.C., she went home.

Jason wanted to go with her, but Katherine said she needed to handle the situation alone. Jason asked her to call him when she got there.

While Katherine was away, Jason went to the store; he bought her a dress, a pair of shoes and another surprise. Jason went to Katherine's parent's house; he spoke with Mr. Roosevelt and handed her Katherine's surprise gift.

He asked Mrs. Roosevelt to call her sisters, and then Mary-ann and Katie, to encourage them to come to the dinner party, which started at 8:00 pm. She also invited all of Katherine's friends and co-workers. Jason called and asked his parents to come, as well.

When Katherine arrived home, she called Jason and told him that she was there and safe at the time. But Thomas wasn't there.

He said to her, "Be careful and call me back when Thomas arrives."

Katherine walked through the house to make sure every-thing was in order before she hung up; she told Jason that the coast was clear; she then hung up the phone.

Katherine noticed two wine glasses on the bedroom night-stand, and the sheets were a bit damp in a few places.

"What's going on?" She asked herself. "Was there another lady staying at the house while I was gone?" However, she didn't see lipstick on the glasses.

She called Thomas, and he answered. She questioned him about the condition of her bedroom. He said, "You've come back home?"

She replied, "Yes."

Thomas told her, "Darling, I am on my way." But he didn't say he had to drop Mindy off first.

Fortunately, he left her house just in time. Thomas made sure Mindy picked up and packed all her belongings every day.

He was also glad to hear from Katherine yet angry because she left him. He and Mindy were headed back to her house.

Katherine stood in the mirror, practicing what to say. Then she asked herself, what am I doing? Say it: I don't love you! What more could he do to you?

The door opened, and Thomas came inside; she heard footsteps rushing towards her. Katherine should have picked up something right then. But Thomas appeared to be excited to see her, and then he started yelling.

He needed to know where she was, and he demanded to know now. Katherine thought, it's none of your business and she was attempted to say it.

However, those were only thoughts. Katherine was afraid, and no matter how brave she felt in front of Jason, she was like a tamed kitten around Thomas.

He came closer to her with one finger pointing toward her face. "I am only going to ask you this question once, and if you don't tell me the truth, I promise I will beat you until no one recognizes you. Did you sleep with Jason?"

Katherine didn't answer. Thomas slapped her and asked her the same question again.

"Did you sleep with Jason?"

She still refused to answer the question. Thomas slapped her harder and demanded to know if she had slept with Jason. Katherine declined to answer the question.

He screamed and gritted his teeth; he grabbed Katherine by the shoulders, he begins shaking her furiously, and then he hit her with the back of his hand. He slapped her again and again.

Katherine started sobbing. "No!"

Thomas slapped her again. Katherine was petrified!

"Thomas, what do you want me to say?"

"I want to know the truth."

"I am telling you the truth."

"Did you let him kiss you or touch your body?" Katherine sighed heavily.

"So that means yes." Thomas took a deep breath.

She knew with his abusive past; he could blow into a rage at any moment.

She was terrified, and she began telling him everything that he wanted to hear. Thomas slapped her several more times until her face was cherry red.

Her phone started ringing; she knew that was her knight protecting his princess. Jason was calling to check on Katherine. She also knew Jason would be on his way if she didn't answer, so she didn't.

Thomas slapped her again and then showed her his gun. "If you ever leave this house again, it will be the last breath you take."

She was listening to him, but she was searching for that opportunity to escape, and as soon as she got the slimmest chance to leave the house, she was going to run and get out of there. Katherine was willing to drop everything and disregard her clothes, the furniture, and the memories.

Katherine and Jason were going to start new lives together, but she had to make it out of here alive first. She just had to wait for that rare moment to run and never look back. Then Thomas said, "Take off your clothes."

"What? No!"

He pointed the gun at her. "You heard me."

Katherine found herself begging and pleading with him again, "Please don't do this."

But his jaw muscles were clamped tight waiting for her to take them off. Katherine didn't know what to do; she didn't have anything near her to protect herself; she slowly pulled her shirt over her head.

She was crying and wondering where Jason was!

Then the doorbell rang; Thomas told her to stay there, but she was waiting for him to open the door so she could run. He set the gun down on the wooden coffee table and answered the door.

Thomas had made a mistake; he cracked the door without seeing who it was. It was Jason. Before Thomas could grab the gun, Jason shoved the door open and raced inside.

Katherine was standing there, shaking and crying with her blouse off. A tear dropped from Jason's eyes.

He told Katherine to put on her shirt and come to him. Jason had rescued her again.

Jason turned.

"Thomas, what is going on?"

"You are just the person I need to talk to; glad you came in."

"I didn't come to talk."

Jason turned slowly. "Katherine, why is your shirt off? Put it back on and come here."

"You move, and I will break your neck." Thomas said.

"Katherine, come here." Jason rubbed his hand down the middle of his face to relax his expression. Katherine started towards Jason. Thomas grabbed her by the shoulder and told her if she took one more step, she would die right there.

Katherine reached out her hand and looked at Jason; tears were pouring down her face. Jason couldn't stand to watch her cry.

Jason closed his eyes; he was getting angrier by the second. But Jason was tearing apart inside. Tears stung the corners of his eyes.

Thomas grinned in scorn at Jason's emotion. "She's not going anywhere." Jason kept staring into Katherine's eyes for about ten seconds.

Her eyes were saying, "I'm tired of suffering. Please help me! I don't care anymore what happens to Thomas."

Jason said, "Your time is up; I am through talking." Moving so quickly he surprised himself, he grabbed Thomas by his left arm and twisted it as if to yank the shoulder socket out.

Thomas screamed and released Katherine's shoulder. He told Katherine, "Get to the car — now!" He held his vice grip on Thomas until Katherine was safe outside. Thomas lunged at Jason, trying to knock him off balance so he could flatten and dominate him.

Jason staggered with force; he felt a sharp pain in his rib cage, but he forced himself to strike Thomas with a hard head-butt to the nose, then a sharp uppercut.

Thomas staggered back, a look of shock and pain flitting across his face. Jason was ready for a slugfest, but Thomas was backing off.

Jason asked Thomas, "How does it feel? I want you to hit me just like you hit Katherine, or do you just like hitting women?" Thomas' nose and lips were bleeding.

Katherine grabbed Jason by the arm and told him, "That's enough." He said, "No, it's not enough. Katherine look in the mirror. Look at your bruises!"

Jason yelled, "It's not enough, Katherine, it's not enough!" He looked at Thomas and said, "You damaged someone I love, and that I cannot forgive." "Please, don't stop me, Katherine," Jason asked.

Katherine saw the pain in Jason's eyes; she walked up to him and kissed him. Then she said, "Let's go." Jason didn't want to stop, but he respected Katherine's wishes."

He told Thomas, "She just saved you; you should thank her." They went to the car. Thomas yelled, "We will meet again."

Jason replied, "I hope so, and I'll be ready, but the next time, Katherine may not be there to save you." Katherine told Jason, "Get in the car." Jason starred at Thomas as he slammed the car door, and then he drove off.

Thomas started ripping Katherine's house apart, destroying expensive paintings and pouring wine on her white carpet.

Thomas had lost control of Katherine and didn't know how to regain it. The more he thought about Katherine lying in Jason's bed, the more in-depth his rage became.

Thomas went into her bedroom; he fell back, his head hit the headboard. What would he do without her, he wondered? Katherine was like a personal diary; she knew hidden secrets about him that no one else knew, not even Mindy.

Thomas convinced that Katherine would never share those secrets. However, he was wrong; her love for Jason was stronger than her fear for him.

Fear had kept Thomas' journal locked for months. But Jason had unlocked his secrets and freed Katherine from mental slavery. Thomas tried to figure out a way to lure Katherine back.

However, he couldn't get into the building where she worked; there were too many security guards there. Jason had increased security around the building.

While Thomas was trying to figure out a plan, Mindy called.

"When are you coming home?"

"Whenever I get there, the next second, minute, day — month...year, I am not in a rush."

"I'll get right to the point. I'm pregnant." Mindy said.

"You're on the pill; it's impossible."

"Did you hear me?" said Mindy.

"I said I was coming home; what more do you want from me?"

Mindy yelled, "That's not what I said...I would love for you to take care of your responsibilities – your children."

"Kids? Are you pregnant? I don't have time for a kid right now; you need to have an abortion."

"No!"

"Do what you like; I'm not taking care of the bastard."

"You're the bastard!" She shouted and hung up the phone.

Thomas knew that if some of the people knew the truth, he would be called a monster for what he had done to Katherine. But he felt an attraction for her that was uncontrollable and how people felt didn't matter.

Thomas had been with Mindy for years, but he'd never experienced that type of need and craving for love. He needed to control Katherine.

Mindy wanted a more stable life for their daughter and the child that she was expecting. Thomas' attention was so focused on Katherine; at first, he didn't comprehend Mindy when she said that she was already pregnant.

His urgency was to get Katherine back. He had a few glasses of liquor, and he finally headed for home. Drinking, driving, and confused was an accident waiting to happen. However, miraculously he made it home safely.

He was quiet for the first time; he had lost his angel, and he wondered if she'd fallen hard for Jason. That was the scariest part to accept.

While driving home, Jason told Katherine, "I promised I would protect you." He took Katherine back to his' house and gave her a dark purple, knee-length, sparkling evening dress, and he asked her to put it on for dinner. They were going out on a date.

Katherine asked, "Where are we going?"

"It's a surprise!"

"I always love your surprises."

Katherine got ready; she lightly brushed on purple eyeshadow and natural lip color. Katherine pinned her hair up in a bun. She put on her heels and left.

Everyone arrived at the ballroom on time. Katherine and Jason came at 8:30. When she walked inside, the lights were turned off; there were several candles lit. Katherine noticed blurred images of people standing around; however, Katherine barely could see her surroundings. She turned around to ask Jason what was going on.

He was kneeling with one knee on the floor. Katherine was thrilled; she had an enormous smile on her face. Her mouth was fixed to say, "Yes."

Her mother turned on the lights. Mr. Roosevelt walked up to Jason and gave him a ring box.

"Oh my," Katherine said. She began crying tears of joy. Jason reached for her hand and placed a white gold, amethyst, and diamond ring on her finger.

"I haven't found anyone who can love me as much as you have," said Jason. "I cannot – no, I don't want to live without you. I have tried, and it broke my heart. I love you! Will you marry me?"

She placed her forehead against his', and she began to cry; she could not believe that she'd found someone to love her despite of her past.

"Of course, Yes!" He chose purple because it stood for royalty, and Katherine was his queen. Jason whispered in her ear, "No sex until marriage, and then I can do what I like to my wife." Katherine giggled.

The room set-up was beautiful; there were lavender roses in the center of each table; a sizeable beautiful chandelier was in the middle of the ceiling. Heart-shaped, purple balloons which proclaimed, "I love you," surrounded the room.

Her family and friends started clapping. The DJ began playing the music, and Jason twirled Katherine around.

They always felt connected on the dance floor. Jason and Katherine pranced around, enjoying their engagement celebration.

Then Sandy received a phone call from Mindy during the celebration. Mindy was on the speakerphone. Sandy went outside to take the call.

She told Mindy that she was at an engagement party, and it was the best ceremony that she had ever attended. So, she would have to call her back later.

Mindy asked Sandy where and who? Sandy told her, "Katherine Roosevelt is engaged to be married, and the party is in the ballroom on Washington Street." Thomas overheard the conversation; he grabbed his gun and ran to his car.

Mindy was yelling his name, "Thomas, Thomas, no Thomas!" But he didn't answer; she heard the car start, and the wheels squealed as he sped off.

Sandy asked Mindy, "What is going on?" Mindy said Katherine and Thomas had recently broken up. Sandy was shocked.

"What are you talking about, Mindy? I never saw them together."

Mindy said, "He was with her at the party; it's a long story." Then Sandy recalled seeing Thomas and Katherine walking next to each other at the college, but it didn't seem like a loving relationship. If she remembered correctly, Thomas always walked behind Katherine; she was never next to him.

That seemed very odd if they were a couple. But Katherine was so miserable that she didn't announce her relationship; only her close friends knew they were together.

Sandy went back inside to enjoy the party. However, she didn't ask her friend, Katherine if any of her and Mindy's conversation was genuine. It might spoil the moment.

However, what Mindy said concerned her. Katherine and Jason were still dancing in the center of the floor. Everyone's eyes aimed at them.

Jason and Katherine had found true love, and everyone in the room felt it in the air, and it was magical. "You Are the Reason" by Colum Scott was playing...

" There goes my heart beating
'Cause you are the reason
I'm losing my sleep
Please come back now

There goes my mind racing
And you are the reason
That I am still breathing"

Then the ballroom door swung open; Jason must've felt that lousy vibe because he leaned his head over and glimpsed Thomas. Everyone turned around; Thomas had a 9mm gun aimed at Katherine's back. People started shouting, "Run."

Jason stared at Thomas, but there was nothing he could do. Thomas was too far away to attempt to disarm.

The security guards pulled out their guns, but it was too late. Thomas fired the weapon, and several bullets were pointed right in the center of Katherine's back. But Jason had to save her one last time, even if it cost his life.

Wrapping his arms around Katherine and holding her head in the palm of his hand, Jason quickly spun her around. She heard a loud pop. A bullet struck Jason; he stumbled and fell on top of Katherine.

The shell pierced him; Jason felt the heat as the bullet penetrated deep into his back. He let go of Katherine. The security guards attacked Thomas and detained him.

He was resisting, trying to tear loose. He kept yelling, "Die sucker, die!" Katherine was sobbing and yelling, "Shut Up."

Jason's eyes closed! He tried to open them, but he could not; all he saw was darkness. He had passed out from the gunshot wound, and he was barely breathing.

His lifeless body was lying on top of Katherine's. He was bleeding heavily.

Tears rolled down Katherine's cheeks. She began screaming hysterically. She couldn't stop yelling out Jason's name.

She was begging him, "Please, wake up! Please wake up; Lord, please, please don't take him. I need him! I love him! Lord, if you take him away, who is going to protect me?"

"Who is going to love me? Jason why didn't you let me die, I can't live without you, wake up, please wake up. Remember those words: I cannot – live without you, you said them to me, and now I am saying them to you! I cannot live without you!"

"Lord, please wake him up. Jason wake up, please, Get up! GET UP!" That's all Katherine kept yelling. No one was able to stop her.

She was on her knees, praying and pleading with God for Jason's life. Please, God, I beg you, do not take him away – don't take him! She cried and held him in her arms for about ten minutes until help came.

By then Jason had gone into shock, his pupils dilated, his heart began beating erratically, his blood pressure dropped, and his breathing came in gasps.

Jason had lost a lot of blood. The bullet was still in his body. One of the deputies tore off Jason's shirt and applied pressure on the wound, attempting to slow down the bleeding.

The ambulance arrived; the paramedics put Jason onto the stretcher and then placed a white sheet across him. Blood quickly covered the sheet.

The paramedics hooked Jason up to the machines. Katherine asked them, "What's happening?" They moved him into the ambulance, and she was permitted to accompany them to the hospital.

Katherine heard the loud siren while she bounced around in the seat. More deputies and detectives arrived, and they hurried inside. Security was still on the phone with dispatch and he informed her that the possible suspect had been apprehended and restrained.

The detective interviewed the witnesses; everyone agreed that Thomas was the shooter. They read Thomas the Miranda and took him into custody.

When the detective asked Thomas if he had shot Jason, he replied:

"Yes, and I will do it again."

They handcuffed Thomas and took him to the local Sheriff's office to interview him and book him. It was Katherine's turn to take care of Jason.

The paramedics took them to Midwestern Hospital, which was across town; it was a more extended metropolitan hospital.

The paramedics informed the resident, and they notified the attending physician of his condition. When they got there, they rushed him to the surgical floor.

Katherine refused to leave his side, but she was not allowed in the surgery room. It was six long agonizing hours of surgery; blood covered the bed.

Katherine paced the waiting room floor, praying and crying out to God. Although she wasn't a praying woman, she needed divine help to detour destiny.

After the doctors finished, the anesthesia wore off, Jason was sedated. The doctor explained to Jason's parents and Katherine that the bullet had missed his subclavian artery by a few inches; the doctor didn't understand, and he couldn't give them a reason why

Jason was still living, other than the fact that fate was on his side.

He explained that they had removed the bullet successfully, but there could be permanent damage. It could take months to see if there were lingering after-effects.

Katherine was frightened, but she was grateful for his life. She couldn't live without Jason, and she didn't want to try. They placed Jason into ICU so that the doctors could keep a close eye on him.

Although he was in a deep sleep, he heard Katherine's cries. In no way could he respond. He lay on the bed in silence.

The crime scene was tightly secured; a detective came to the hospital to interview the two primary witnesses.

He had questioned many who were at the ballroom, except Katherine and, of course, Jason who was unable to speak.

The detective shook Katherine's hand. "My name is Detective Moore; I am here to investigate the shooting. I need to interview you, and I need a taped statement."

"I'm Katherine — the patient, Jason Taylor, is my fiancé."

"How is he doing?"

"Well, the doctor said that the surgery was successful.

"He's still alive for now; that is all that matters to me."

"I'm pleased to hear that! I know that you are experiencing trauma, but I need to ask you some questions to find out what exactly occurred at the ballroom."

Katherine nodded. "It happened so fast! I didn't see anything; I only heard what was transpiring."

"What happened in your own words?"

"Jason and I were dancing on the dance floor. I heard a commotion, and then the door opened. Someone in the crowd yelled, 'run." Tears fell from Katherine's eyes. "Excuse me."

Katherine paused, wiping her eyes and runny nose. "Then I heard a loud popping sound. Jason had spun me around. I could not figure out what was happening, and then suddenly, he fell on top of me. He was bleeding profusely.

That's all I remember."

The detective went to the nurse's station to get a box of Kleenex and then came back and handed Katherine one. "It's ok, from what I've gathered so far, everyone's details are coinciding. It appears that Jason took the bullet for you. Thomas was aiming at your back. Why would he want to shoot you?"

She wiped her tears. "Who knows, Thomas – he's a lunatic, and it's a long story. "But I am not surprised by the shooting."

"Why not?"

"I am a victim of domestic violence."

"Did you ever report the abuse?"

"No."

"Why not?"

"It's complicated!"

"Well ma'am, we have a man lying in a hospital bed with a bullet in his back; complicated is not a good enough answer."

"Well, part of me cared; he always seemed sorrowful afterward, and he gave me lavishing gifts. I was also afraid. Thomas is a well-known attorney; I thought that everyone would take his side."

"Ma'am the only side that I am on or interested in is the truth. I'm strictly here to find out what happened and get another scumbag off the street. I need you to tell me everything that occurred."

Katherine told it all, not holding back on anything. Finally, she said, "Thomas wanted revenge! He has told Jason and me repeatedly to watch our backs because he was going to kill us."

"Why didn't you call the police?"

"Everyone told me to, but I thought he was bluffing, and it was another one of his controlling episodes to force me to come home. Besides, as I said, he is an attorney, he worked so hard for his degree. I never thought that he would do something so foolish to lose it."

"You said you weren't surprised about the shooting, and you thought he was bluffing? We are depraved humans, some more than others, and a prestigious career or who you are doesn't always exclude you from committing a high crime. So, have people witnessed the beatings?"

"No! It always happened when it was just us."

"Did you go to the doctor?"

"No, I was ashamed and intimidated. I did not want anyone to know that I was living with such a monster."

"Well, I did go to the hospital a few times, but I said it was an accident."

"Did anyone witness it? Do you have any pictures or any evidence?"

"My family and Jason saw the bruises, but no one witnessed the beatings!"

"I have spoken with your family, and they did confirm that there were cuts and bruises, they were unsure of how it happened. They did say that you eventually told them that Thomas was the aggressor and they believed you."

"He was."

"How long have you and Thomas been dating?"

"More than a year."

"More than a year?" he asked, "You don't know exactly how long?"

"Does it matter? After being abused for months; I finally decided to leave — especially considering the last incident. I wanted to be happy and look at what it cost me."

"I went out of town with Jason so that I could begin healing physically and mentally. Thomas called me at least a hundred times, begging me to come home. When I refused, he threatened to kill me – kill us. I knew one day that I would die, but I never imagined Jason taking my place. He was only trying to help me escape."

The detective nodded. "I'm sure there are more questions; therefore, I will call you if I need you."

He left a card with her and asked her to call him as soon as Jason woke up.

After the detective left, Sandy came to the room to speak with Katherine. She told Katherine that she had something important to say to her, and she felt guilty she hadn't spoken sooner.

Katherine said, "As long as it's not more bad news."

Sandy started talking fast and then she apologized. Katherine couldn't understand what she was saying. Katherine asked her to slow down.

"Why is it your fault?" said Katherine.

"I told Mindy that I was at your engagement party."

"Who the hell is Mindy? The lady at the party, what does she have to do with Jason or me?"

"She said that you were dating her boyfriend, Thomas?"

"What, I'm confused –... wait a minute. Are you telling me that Thomas has a girlfriend?"

"Yes, her name is Mindy, and they have a daughter together. Thomas is also expecting a second child, I think."

"I have to sit down; I cannot believe this. Thomas has made my life miserable –a living hell, and now you are telling me he has a girlfriend; a child and they're expecting another one?"

"Yes, he does!"

"No, he doesn't."

"Yes, Katherine he does, I have known them for years. The party that I invited you to, it was for Mindy."

"I understand now."

"But I never saw Mindy and Thomas together."

Katherine was becoming more enraged by the second.

"Because you came late and then left early; it was in the middle of the party, by then they were probably mingling with other people."

"But I met with him a few times on campus, and no one said a word."

"Met him on campus? Katherine, he is not enrolled in our college; he goes to the one across town. I saw him walking behind you a few times, but I thought maybe he was working on a project, now I wonder if that project was you."

Sandy paused. "I promise you, I never noticed anything out of the ordinary; yes, maybe a few brows rose when I saw him at the school, but nothing that alarmed me. He could have been speaking in the auditorium; he is a mentor. Thomas does speeches, and he has a friend that goes there. I certainly didn't see this coming."

"Now, you're telling me that he doesn't go to the same school?" asked Katherine. I must vomit, where is the trash can? Was I that naive or desperate for a man that I never saw any of these clues? This entire situation is outlandish! I don't care how many years that you have known Thomas or Mindy — all of this is a lie. Why would you purposely hurt me, when all I have been was a friend to you? Why would you lie to me?"

Katherine began yelling, and then the nurses said, "Please, quiet it down or leave."

"This man raped me, he hit me, kicked me, slapped me, and when I left, he retaliated by trying to kill me, spat Katherine. I tried to injure myself – lastly, he shot my fiancé, and you have the nerve to tell me that he has a girlfriend?"

People passing in the hallway turned and looked at them.

"I can't deal with this, not now!"

Sandy hung her head. "I'm sorry!"

"Sandy, do you know how many times I heard that? I am sorry that I had to beat you! I am sorry I had to cut you! I am sorry I had to punch you; it's like a broken record."

Sandy said, "I will talk to you later."

"No, let's talk now. Yes, I'm furious because this is too much for me to handle. I have been dating this man for a year and a half, and no one tells me the fact that he's dating? So, yes, I am outraged! Sandy, there has to be a mix-up; it's impossible, and you have made a mistake."

Katherine pulled up her left and right sleeve and pointed at her arms. "Look at these scars – look," she roared. "Look at My Scars."

"Shhh," said a nurse. Katherine lowered her voice.

"Let me lift my shirt; this scar here is when he stuck a knife against my chest and pushed it until it cut into my skin. Then he said, 'I should've pressed it into your heart and then watched you while you bled to death.'

This one — I got this other one because I came home late. Would you like to see more? And you tell me that this man has a girlfriend. How many scars does she have?"

Sandy could only mumble in embarrassment.

"How many let us fucking talk, Sandy."

Sandy said, "None."

"I thought not. My life is depressing, and everything that I thought was real has been a fucking lie. And things keep getting worse! None – she has no scars? Well, I guess she should be happy that he never truly loved her! Congratulate her!"

Tears dropped from Katherine's eyes. "I apologize," said Sandy, "but I just learned of this tonight that you and Thomas were dating. It was a surprise. I had told Mindy years ago to leave him. It is not Thomas' first rodeo, he's cheated on her numerous times, and there have been several women coming in and out of his life. But some of these things you're telling me are outrageous."

"You told her to leave because he cheated. Is that all he did to her? Well, he cheated, raped, and beat me. You say what I'm saying is 'Outrageous'? Let me take off this makeup and show you outrageous." Katherine sighed. "This anger that I have is not your fault; this fight is not your battle. Thank you for telling me, but I have to go!" She gave Sandy a quick hug.

"I wanted to tell you what Mindy said, but you and Jason were so happy."

"You are right; I was so happy!" said Katherine. "Let me call Thomas; he's in jail, I forgot."

Katherine left the hospital and went to the Sheriff's office. They were interviewing Thomas. She asked the detective if she could speak to him. He told her that the judge usually awards a no-contact order; she asked him for a few seconds.

He said, "No."

Katherine wanted to know how much of this was true. Hours later, her phone rang. She answered, and it was a prepaid collect call from jail. Thomas had contacted her through a third party.

Thomas said, "Hey, Katherine, I only have a few minutes."

"That's all I need."

"I miss you!"

"You tried to kill me!"

"As the saying goes, if I can't have you, no one will."

"I don't want to discuss that…are you dating a woman named Mindy?"

"Who told you?"

"That's your answer?"

"What would you like me to say? I knew you would eventually find out."

"I would like for you to tell the truth, liar. But, never mind, you disgust me, and you are not worth getting angry over. From this day forward, stay away from Jason and me!"

"Katherine, the only thing that saddens me is that he didn't die."

"I hate you!"

"And I love you!"

"Excuse me?" Do you love me? Is that what you call this sickness? I can't deal with this right now; I need to take care of Jason." She hung up the phone.

Thomas yelled, "Come back to this phone." He called her back, but she didn't answer. He left a voice message saying, "I love you, and I will be back to finish the job!" Katherine ignored the message but kept it just in case it would eventually constitute evidence.

For days, Katherine stayed at the hospital next to Jason. Someone up above must have heard her cries because Jason finally woke up, and he whispered, "Why are you crying?"

Katherine looked over, and Jason was trying to focus his eyes.

She told him, "Because, I thought you were dead."

Jason said, "I promised you, I will be here forever, and a day, and I am going to keep my promise."

Jason reached his hand up to Katherine's face and wiped the tears from her eyes. Then he closed his eyes again, but Katherine had hope that he would recover.

The next morning, Jason was fully alert. He called out to Katherine. She said, "I'm right here; I've hardly left your room since the incident."

Jason told her that he had something to say to her: "I heard you yelling my name,"

"Huh?"

"I believe it was the night of the shooting," he said. "I felt like someone shot me down, and then I felt pain. I heard you crying. The pain in your voice was devastating, so, I fought – I couldn't die. I was praying and asking God not to take me away from you! God and you are the reasons that I am alive."

After Jason was well enough to converse clearly, he called Detective Moore, and the man returned to the hospital. Jason didn't want to press any charges against Thomas.

However, he asked the detective what he had to do to make sure Thomas stayed out of their lives forever. Since that's all Jason wanted, the detective suggested that he get a restraining order upon Thomas' release.

However, the deputy still had to make a report, and the case was out of his hands. Jason asked Katherine to call his parents into the room. He told her to contact everyone and let them know that he was doing fine. Then he instructed the hospital not to accept any visitors except for Katherine.

CHAPTER 17

D etective Moore -

What happened?

"Not without an attorney?

"Okay!" I said as I quickly walked out of the interview room. I closed the heavy door.

I bit my teeth against my bottom lip. I have never felt so much pain – rage before.

I paced back and forth, looking down at the shaded carpet. I yelled loudly and pointed at the steel door, this scumbag shoots an honest man, and then he asks me for an attorney; it frustrates me to let that filth make a phone call.

I finally unraveled and walked back into the interview room. I slammed the phone on the table.

Deep inside, it bothered me to know that he may get away with this crime, and the jerk showed no remorse for what he had done.

I handed him the phone 'politely' since it is my civic duty, and he smirks. Anger was seeping deeper within me. My public mission was about to go straight through the window. However, I remained calm and professional.

The prissy attorney finally gets here, and then she asked in an icy tone, "Where is my client?"

I stared and wondered how she could defend him? However, I walked the zealous attorney into the room. Her black suit freshly pressed. She sits her brand name briefcase on the floor, and we all sat around the table.

Now, tell me what happened – Thomas?

"You tell me. You are the detective who interviewed everyone?" said Thomas.

I want to hear your side.

"Why, when you have already made a judgment call."

I looked at his heartless lawyer and said as an attorney; you already know my job is to investigate the facts and if the evidence is leading to a judgment call well —, I looked at Thomas – oh well.

"So, you are judging me?"

Am I judging you? I shake my head…no, the facts are judging you, God – judges you, the twelve jurors they judge you. I only obtain the actualities.

"Who truth is you referring to that tramp— Katherine's statement, or that fraidy-cat Jason reality, they both are liars."

Well, tell me the truth, Thomas.

"The truth is Jason came to our home to kill me. I do not understand why he is so angry; Katherine is my woman. Did he tell you that he tried to kill me? Did he tell you those – facts or did she, since we are collecting the proof."

Did you know that Katherine dated Jason in high school?

"You are a liar! She made love to me?"

You are insane; you raped her.

"That harlot asked for it, and I gave it to her. Ask her?"

She has her version of the truth, and you have your delusions. She made it very clear that she loved Jason. I guess you did not know that fact. Katherine and Jason were in love, — she loved him. You were a ricochet, a small reflection of Jason. They were – destined to get married.

I taunted Thomas. I depended on his obsession for Katherine to force him into losing control.

He slammed the palm of his hands against the table and roared while he stared at me, "You Are A Liar. But I get it, you desire her too. Did the harlot seduce you too?"

I smiled and then said your aching heart wishes I was

lying. However, I have no reason to be untruthful.

His attorney whispered into his ear, "I advise you to calm down." Then she said, "My client and I are finished."

I will escort him back to his cell, I said. I remained peaceful as we walked down the long, stone hallway. We stopped at cell block G.

I pulled the steel bars open, Thomas still handcuffed. I removed the cuffs. He walked over to the stone bed and sat on the edge. His eyes were frosty and locked on me.

I wondered what was he thinking? I could feel the reserved, abhorrence vibes as I walked away.

Thomas –

Lonely, abandoned, and imprisoned in this cage with strangers. I am feeling hopeless – assurance …hmm, a shadow. I need to escape from this pit before it gobbles me.

I blame Jason for taking everything from me. Notably, the most important thing, my beautiful Katherine.

Shivering and sitting in this prison surrounded by concrete walls and bars, safeguarded from my beloved. I miss Katherine…so much, and I know she is missing me too.

I fathomed more and more – how will I live without her. I question, who will look over her until I am free? Certainly not, – that weakling who she eventually marries? I am enraged!

Since my arrest, I have been able to think much more precise, and I am confident that the boy has programed Katherine's mind.

He brainwashed her into marrying him and now – that I am in jail, I trust that he has forced her to yield to him. That punk is the one who should be behind these slavery bars – not me.

It's subzero and isolated in here, the thick, cracked walls gazing at me every second of the day. I stare back, and it seems like the walls are talking to me.

"Look at you – incarcerated, while Katherine is sleeping

in another man's arms – kissing and making love to him." I hate that punk!

The people screaming from the other cells as if they are insane, I do not belong in this place. I punch the walls – to shut them up. My knuckles bleed as if I was pummeling Katherine's cheekbone.

That boy earnt everything he got, including the bullet. "Are you remorseful for what you have done," the detective asked?

Ha! I am more regretful for what I did not accomplish – sending him to meet his death angel.

I promise I am going to kill that boy the first opportunity I sprawl. He is going to remember me and then regret that he ever laid his vile eyes on my woman.

He unearths me, especially when he watches Katherine as if he is hunting her. She is so vulnerable.

I indulge in setting a trap for my prey. Jason will learn that a chicken has no business coop up in the fox's pen. He will witness hate on the verge of drudgery.

Detective Moore will pay for his lies as well – implying that Katherine loved that grease parrot. She would never sink so low.

I will kill Detective Moore too if I get the chance. The two of them were on my assassination list, and I will not play by the rules.

They have forced me to become this astringent person. Sitting on the bed rocking and rocking, I am going crazy, speaking to the wall, banging my head on my lap, scratching, and rambling.

Katherine is the only person who can rescue my incapacitated mind. The nightmares are tormenting me, and so are these cell bars.

The lights go off; I remember freedom beyond the bars. Making love to Katherine for the first time inside the bathtub, talk about great memories.

I promise when am finally freed from this hell, I have plans to finish the job and make sure Jason never sees Katherine again. I call her phone relentlessly and like before; she doesn't answer. She knows that I hate it when she doesn't answer me. It only annoys me more!

Mindy –

I went to the jailhouse to visit Thomas; I looked into his eyes; something about them seemed odd. They were dilated and tranquilized; they looked as if they were dead.

I tried to kiss him. However, he shoved me away. Then he asked me, have you seen Katherine?

"What?"

For the first time I realized, he does not love me. I threw my arms up and said it is over. I don't believe he even heard me, or he did not care.

I walked away, and he did not stop me until our daughter said: "Daddy!"

"Where are you going?"

"MINDY," he shouted.

I immediately stopped; tears drowned my eyes. Thomas sedated by Katherine; he looked at me and said: "I need you to do something for me."

What – anything?

If I mail you a letter, can you take it to her?

Are you serious?

"Yes!"

My eyes blinked, I closed them and said: "of course, my darling."

I can hear, "Say Something" by A Great Big World and Christina Aguilera; some of the words were ringing in my ear:

"And I will swallow my pride
You're the one that I love
And I'm saying goodbye

Say something, I'm giving up on you
And I'm sorry that I couldn't get to you

And anywhere, I would have followed you"

"Give Katherine a letter?" I asked.

"Give Katherine a letter," he said.

"Give Katherine a letter?" That is what he said to me. My world halted and came to an end by those few words.

He desired to express how much he loves her. Well, do you like me, I asked?

"Yes, but it is a different type of love," he answered!

What is a different type of love, I asked? You either love me, or you love her, which is it?

"It's different Mindy; I am in love with her."

I love this conversation, and I despise you both!

What about the baby? I asked.

Thomas walked up to me and whispered in my ear.

"What about you and that bastard that you are carrying, it's not mines. It should have been Katherine's baby."

Why would you say that to me and about our child? I whelp.

"I told you to have an abortion; I do not desire another child from a slut, and then you disobeyed me and had that kid. It does not change my feelings. My soul is dead without Katherine. When are you going to recognize that?"

How could you hurt me like this?

"How could you hurt me, you brought it on yourself when you got pregnant. I do not love you! Don't you see me bouncing from woman to woman? I was searching for love, and I discovered it when I saw Katherine for the first time."

My voice trembled, why would you say that?

"Mindy, I slept with you because Katherine would not make love to me. However, that special night – was a night to remember. Not like that rubbish sex that I have with you. It was the greatest feeling that I have ever felt. She yelled out for more, and I gave it to her."

You disgust me!

"No, you disgust me – you harlot."

I am leaving you.

"Wait, I apologize. I love you." He kissed her on the lip.

I needed to hear those words, I said and then I replied I love you too! I felt relieved when I listened to those three words, "I love you!" Thomas knew how to calm me.

Thomas was beginning to feel deserted, the exact feeling Katherine felt. Thomas trapped inside a confined space, which he could not escape, stranded and powerless.

Where he had no authority, he could not control the guards, bedtime, or recreation time. However, Thomas ruled Mindy. She was the only thing left that he could manipulate. Someone had to take Katherine's place since she was gone.

Thomas looked into Mindy's eyes; he saw that same fearful gaze in Katherine's eyes. He felt an intense pleasure when they cried. "Why – I feel this way, he asked himself." He felt deep happiness when they suffered, a cheerfulness that eased his pain.

Mindy hated Katherine, as much as Thomas hated Jason. She also hated Thomas for loving Katherine.

She was driving home, crying and asking herself, "Why does Katherine keep interfering in our lives?" Tabby begins crying with her mother. Don't cry, baby! Mommy is okay! That woman will pay for hurting daddy and I. Mindy was starting to plot – how to get rid of her. Katherine needed to go.

Thomas was scheming as well on how to get rid of Jason. Both of their desires for love were their inspirations, the blueprint for their plot.

Mindy's eyes were red, her forehead wrinkled and her nose – expanded, possessed by something or someone perhaps passion.

CHAPTER 18

Three months later, Jason wounds healed completely. Katherine called Katie and asked her to plan the wedding. Katie came over, and she brought the scrapbook that Walter had made with her.

Katie –

Jason and Katherine were in love. They shared their ideas of an extraordinary wedding with Walter and me, and I desired to plan their beautiful wedding. Walter and I shared details of the wedding with one another.

Walter was a unique artist. He loved painting, drawing, and creating unique crafts.

Each day in class, I shared Katherine's wedding ideas with him, and each day he painted an image of the wedding in a sketchbook, which I later learned that he had secretly made for me.

When he completed the book, he handed it to me. I was surprised; it was magnificent!

It was an old, worn, red scrapbook with white lace fabric wrapped around it. Walter tied a velvety red ribbon in the shape of a bow on the top right-hand corner of the book.

There were several red bush roses in the shape of a heart towards the center. In the middle of the roses was a large glass heart-shaped pendant. Engraved two different harmonies, but one beat.

I felt like the design meant something more than Katherine's favorite flower, her prom skirt material, or memories. But what did it mean? Why was the glass stone in the middle of the roses? What did it symbolize? I asked Walter.

"It represents Katherine's heart."

How sweet is that?

Then Walter pointed at my chest and said, "If Katherine chooses the wrong man; her life – her heart would be just like the glass stone. If it falls against a hard surface; it may break or shatter."

I was unable to fathom why he said that, but the book was incredible and an excellent memoir.

I explained every detail of the wedding, and Walter captured it piece by piece. Katherine's vision of a dream wedding was described precisely: ballroom gowns, white carriages and horses, white doves, and colorful roses.

I wanted to bring Katherine's wedding into existence. However, I never shared the book with anyone. If they were going to be married, I wanted the wedding to be an awesome surprise.

Katherine –

Alliance, I had met Maryann Thompson and Katie Randall at school. We became best friends.

However, I was the big guru of the group and the nerdy one of the three; I had high hopes and soaring spirits. I enjoyed writing.

Maryann was the most talented one; she enjoyed singing, dancing, and playing the saxophone. Maryann was an incredible artist with a fantastic voice. She composed songs with so much compassion, as though she felt your sorrows and pleasures.

I had written several songs, and Maryann sang them with a soft-pitched, but a loving and robust voice, which captivated the crowd at school. The words of the song and Maryann's appealing voice made tears flood from the audience's eyes.

She was able to empathize with the crowd, and when she danced, it was flawless: ballet, modern dance, hip-hop or the samba. It did not matter; she was well overly qualified.

Have you ever just listened to instrumental saxophone music? The sounds that Maryann made with her saxophone made you fall in love with the music, and it was magical.

Specific songs hit your soul like a semi-truck. That was Maryann playing that saxophone.

Katie worked at the school as a secretary before and after classes, hoping she could become a wedding planner one day. After all, knowing how to schedule appointments and ordering supplies were part of the job requirements.

I kept imagining myself getting married to my mystery man after I finished establishing a career for myself. I was going to have one of the most beautiful weddings ever.

I was saving my body for him, I didn't know anything about lovemaking, but whatever it was, he was the person that I wanted to do it with for the rest of my life. I kept visualizing Jason and me kissing and touching one another.

I shared all my wedding dreams with Katie and Maryann, which inspired Katie to become a wedding planner.

Katie and Katherine looked through the book together; it was perfect. The bride-to-be wanted a ballroom gown just like the one that was in the book.

Katherine searched numerous bridal stores, trying to find the best one for her, the one Walter sketched.

It was the dress that would blow Jason's mind. But Katherine couldn't spot that dress.

Katherine's sister, Brittany looked at the drawing, and told her that she would make it for her, but she needed more time — at least six months. Katherine paused; it took over three months for Jason to heal; now, she had to wait again.

Katherine took a deep breath. "The wedding has to be delayed."

Brittany said, "Just for a little while."

Shelley Jenkins

"For you, but for me, it seems like an eternity."

"I promise every minute that you wait will be worth it," said Brittany. "Besides, what is better than getting married in the same month and day that you met? Talk about memories!" Katherine grimaced. "I have some awful ones."

Brittany said, "The bad ones you'll forget." Brittany took Katherine's measurements as well as those of the maid of honor, and the bridesmaids. Brittany wrote the sizes down and immediately began making the dresses.

Katie and Katherine sent invitations to the guests, inviting them to an extravagant wedding. The invitees were asked to wear gowns and tuxedos.

Katie asked Maryann to sing and play the saxophone and teach Katherine how to dance. Samantha was going to play the piano.

They had six months to get everything together, and they needed to find an incredible outdoor wedding venue with a garden. Somewhere secluded, but stylish.

They hired a florist to help set up the rose garden. Katie looked around and found the perfect venue. It was going to be a spring wedding when the flowers were beginning to bloom. Nothing was better than an Easter wedding with pastel colors.

The date was getting closer. Katherine was becoming more and more excited. Katie had gotten everything together, and she was ready for the show to begin.

Jason and the fellows had picked the spot-on white slim fit tuxedo with gray, silver silk jacket and tie.

Katherine's sisters and her friends were doing the final preps the morning before the big day, Tuesday, April 24, 2012.

It was finally here. It was not going to be a traditional wedding.

The ushers seated the guests in their assigned areas in the middle of the field across from Maryann. The brides and groom's parents and grandparents were there.

There was a combination of white flowers; rose bushes, hollyhocks, orchids, lilies, carnations, and white cherry blossom trees.

The white carriage was sitting in the middle of the venue next to a small bridge; you could hear the water flowing from the river below the bridge. A large crowd was there.

The ladies wore formal wedding dresses, and the men wore tuxedos. Katherine had five bridesmaids, and Katie was the maid of honor; they all wore white lace tops with a deep v-cut, which showed their bare backs, the scraps were thin, lavender belts, and silver mermaid skirts. Their bouquets composed of white carnations and lavender roses.

There were five groomsmen; they had on gray silk tuxedos. The ring bearer was Walter. Katherine was overwhelmed with excitement; the bridesmaids tried to keep her relaxed.

Two minutes before the wedding began. Katherine became frightened; wondering if she made the right decision.

"I don't know," Katherine said.

Katie said, "Katherine, you have been waiting for this day ever since high school, and now that it's that moment you are saying, "I'm not ready?"

"A lot has happened."

"We both know that Jason loves you, endlessly."

"What about the rape? I'm giving him less than he deserves."

Katherine, the rape is unfortunate, but if you want a successful marriage, you will have to overcome the victim role. It's time to move on – move forward."

"What if the marriage doesn't work out?"

Katie sighed. "What if it does? Now stop making excuses and go. Your groom is waiting for you."

Katherine was wondering if the wedding was going to happen. Things were too perfect; she never felt so complete, she had to be dreaming. She was expecting something to happen and ruin her big day.

Katie and Maryann were whispering, "Breathe and step, breathe and step, breathe and step." Katherine finally walked out; it was silent. Katie walked next to her for support.

Everyone was staring at her, as the guests stood up. Katherine saw Jason standing in the middle of the bridge; she paused and barely took a step, and then she stopped. She was nervous and afraid!

She had on a tight white sweetheart beaded see-through corset and a ballroom bottom that puffed out at the waistline. Her accessories of choice were pearls — Katherine's bouquet made of white roses, lilies, and large beads.

Jason dropped his head for the first time in his life; he was excited but anxious. He kept saying under his breath, "You can do this."

Katherine was crying, she took another half step, and she stopped again. Katherine wondered if she was doing the right thing.

The photographer stopped taking pictures until she got herself together. Katherine started thinking.

"How does Jason honestly feel about being with a rape victim?" It seemed like each step for her became more challenging. Jason was looking at her and coaching her from the afar – one step at a time sweetheart, one step at a time.

Katherine took one step and then another until she reached her mother and father, who was waiting for her. Katherine's mother and father continued to walk her towards the groom. When she got there, she paused for a few minutes, and then Mrs. Roosevelt murmured, "it's okay."

Katherine took another step, and the photographer resumed taking pictures. Mrs. Roosevelt kept whispering 'one step at a time.'

Katherine reached the bridge, the bottom covered with rose petals, and the arch surrounded by flowers. She walked between two images of angels towering over her. A carriage sat at the end of the bridge, waiting for the bride and groom.

Jason stood there waiting with his head dropped; she reached out her hand and lifted it when she got closer to him.

The guests were waving and smiling at Katherine. Tears filled Jason's eyes. Katherine's mother gave her away and hugged her, and then she embraced Jason. She placed Katherine's hand on top of Jason's hand, and she walked away.

"You are beautiful!" he said.

"And you are handsome!"

"Are you ready to do this?"

"Yes, I am!"

Jason and Katherine walked hand in hand to a white Cinderella carriage, which carried them through a beautiful rose garden and into the venue. They kept crying; she was still hesitant about the marriage, especially with everything that was going on.

White roses, hollyhock swallowtail garden seeds, and chairs stood throughout the site. Jason stepped out of the wagon and walked around it to Katherine. He held her hand while she stepped out of the carriage. Katherine's dress was perfect. She and Jason trod white carpet covered with white rose petals. Her dress dragging against the carpet.

There were two flower girls, one of them was dropping additional pink rose petals, and the other one tossed the leaves in the air. The music started, and her sister played a white grand piano that sat in the middle of the garden.

Maryann played a white saxophone, "Thousand Years" song by Christina Perri:

"One step closer
Time stands still
Beauty she is
I will be brave
I will not let anything take away
What's standing in front of me
Every breath, every hour has come to this
One step closer."

It was time for the royal entrance; Jason and Katherine were nervous.

Katherine was on the left; her father and her mother greeted her again, and then they guided her down the aisle.

At the same time, Jason's mother and father stood beside him, and they all walked down the aisle together — that was one of the not-so-traditional parts.

It seemed as if everyone was crying; it was an extraordinary moment for Katherine and Jason. They'd finally found their true love.

Jason stood straight, and Katherine's veil hung down her face.

They escorted the groom and the bride under the wedding arch made of branches, vines, and flowers. The minister was waiting for Katherine and Jason.

The photographer took pictures of them while they stood next to a cherry blossom tree that was in the rose garden.

The minister said, "You may be seated." For the vow exchange, Katie and Maryann stood beside Katherine.

"I Jason take you to be my wife, best friend, lover, and queen and I offer you my solemn vow to be there for you every day."

"Katherine, I promise to love you and only you, every single day! I promise I will cherish you forever and a day! I promise to be there for you for the rest of my life, even when everyone else has turned their backs on you and I will talk for you when you cannot speak!"

"I promise to honor and protect you with all my might, especially when you're not strong enough to fight! I vow to carry the weight on my shoulders! I vow to be your husband and your husband only. I vow to wipe away your tears and never cause you any! I vow to open your doors and take off your clothes!" The crowd laughed.

Katherine shook her head and said to him, "I, Katherine, take you to be my hero, my king, my lover, my best friend and my cook. [Crowd laughs again] I offer you my solemn vow to be there for you forever and a day. Jason, I vow to be your wife, and only yours!"

"I promise to hold you tight every single night! I vow to care for you when you're sick and when you're well! I vow to love you, and love you, and love you more, some more, and more! And I vow to keep my clothes on!"

The crowd was enjoying this. Walter brought the ring; Katherine's final dream was coming true. Jason slid the large diamond ring on her finger. She waved the back of her hand toward the crowd, and they applauded.

The minister said, "Dearly beloved, we are gathering this day to witness this man and woman join together in holy matrimony." Tears filled Jason and Katherine's eyes. "Does anyone here object to the marriage?" Then he said, "By the power invested in me by the state of Washington, I now pronounce you, Jason and Katherine, man and wife, you may kiss the bride."

They lit the candle, and released the doves, and then they kissed, kissed, and kissed. Afterward, everyone walked to the reception.

In the reception hall, the center table was long and square; it seated about thirty people. Then there were five rectangular tables attached, which sat approximately six people per table. Katherine's family and closest friends were sitting at the rectangle table next to them. White roses, combined with other flowers, trailed in the center of the table.

Five lit chandeliers sat right above the square table, and five tall crystal vases shaped like wine glasses with large candles sat underneath each light.

The glass vases had trees of white roses lying between them. Expensive dinnerware sat on the tables.

Several round tables were on each side of the square table. They sat about ten people per meal. A white weeping china doll rose tree was in the center of each roundtable. Candles and roses were ordered and placed on the tables.

A tower of different flavored cupcakes and other desserts were on the table next to the wall. There was also a table with assorted white candies lined across it.

The eight-tiered white cake sat on a glass candle stand; it had pink rose petals. Each layer represented a year that they had spent together.

There were arrangements made for dinner; confectioners set up the dinner tables. They assigned each guest a seat.

The caterers came to each person that was seated to serve

them a memorable dinner. It was their first dance as man and wife. Maryann sang a begging song, "Let's Dance," and Samantha played the piano. The words to the song were:

Oh baby, oh baby,
I fell in love –
Baby, baby, I fell in love
With you

Oh baby, baby, baby, oh baby –
Baby, I fell in love
With you

But you left me – you left me
And you crushed me –
Baby, you crushed my heart baby
Now I'm crying and my hearts breaking
Baby, baby, baby I need you baby
Please, Please baby
Come back home
You destroyed my world baby
I can't sleep – baby, and I can't make it without you

Please come back to me
Please come back to me
Please, baby, remove this pain,
Oh baby, please baby, wipe away these tears,
  Please, Please, please baby repair my heart
Show me, love baby
I need – I need
Your love so much – baby
Oh Baby, oh baby, I need your love baby

Please baby, please
I ask you for one more dance
One more dance baby
Us baby, hand and hand
One more dance baby

Us one on one
Baby, baby – us heart to heart
Oh-oh baby, us soul to soul baby

Let's danced
Forever-more
Let us dance baby forever baby
Baby forever
Just one more dance baby

Baby, baby, baby I fell in love
I fell in love
With you

Oh, baby,
I love you more and more
Each day

Let's dance baby
Let's dance baby
Baby, baby let's dance

The DJ played more love songs, and everyone danced. Dancing was the best part of their relationship. It was when they bonded the most.

Their love had begun, and it became stronger on the dance floor. When they danced, they held each other tightly. As usual, Jason and Katherine lost focus on everything around them — including the guests.

When Katherine spun in circles, her problems seemed to disappear magically. Jason held Katherine's soft body in his arms as he waltzed across the floor.

Her body pressed against his. Katherine smile was enormous. She was happier than she ever been, and it was an incredible day for her.

Then "Diamonds" by Rihanna played next. That's what she was to Jason, "A diamond in the sky." Katherine had married the man of her dreams, and it was excellent. As always, they didn't want the dance to end.

Jason refused to take Katherine on a honeymoon until they spent their first night together at new her home and in his bed wrapped in his arms, making love together for the first time repeatedly.

Katherine tasted like the finest chocolate. Jason's gentle touches made her cry out in pleasure, and his kisses were drugging her.

Katherine –

I got up to use the bathroom. I turned on the light and then looked at the mirror. I stood there gazing into the mirror, who am I beyond the make-up, the heartbreaks, the tears. I still could not figure it out.

However, the one thing that I am sure of is my feelings for Jason, I love him – and nothing would never come between us again.

I have reached new heights. Since Jason came into my life, I am no longer afraid to look at my beautiful face or hear the doors slam or listen to footsteps walking towards me.

It is our honeymoon at home; I lie in bed beside Jason and stare at him while he sleeps. I pondered, "What did he ever see in me?"

He wakes up, and he smiles at me, my heart smiles back. I kiss his lips and then stare into his eyes.

He pulls my bare body closer to his firm chest. His arms wrapped around me tightly, and then he kisses me intensely on the neck and between my breast and giving me love bites.

He traces my body with his lips as if he was painting a portrait of me with his tongue. Nothing is better than making love to my husband.

I'm laying her cuddled in Jason's arms staring into his eyes, kissing him as his penis penetrates deep inside of me. I close my eyes because my feelings are overtaking me as he strokes me gently.

Jason –

Katherine was the one person that was worthy of spending an eternity loving. When we got home, I carried Katherine straight to my bedroom; I smelled the scent of her perfume as I grappled her nipples inside my mouth.

I loved touching and licking every inch of her curvy body. Making love to her for the first time as husband and wife was the most beautiful moment of my life.

Katherine –

I hunger to lay in his arms. However, we must go on our honeymoon. I get up and then fill the bathtub with warm water.

I put one leg in the tub. Jason comes and stands behind me and wraps his arms around my waist, I feel his erected penis against my buttocks, and I lean my head back into his chest.

He held my breast in his hands. I pulled away. Then I put the other leg into the bathtub. He tried to join me, and he won.

I dried off then and put on a purple bell sleeve dress, which hugged my body. I styled my hair in a bun and then put on a pair of glasses.

Jason showered and then put on a black suit. He stood beside me and stared at me, "You look beautiful," he said, and you are handsome, I said.

We were in the mood again; however, we had to get out of this house. I will drive, and you can ride with me, on my lap if you like he said, I prefer seats, I said. I had finally found my happily ever after, I assumed.

Made in the USA
Columbia, SC
04 September 2020